"If only we could go backward in time!"

Kyle's eyes were shamelessly desirous, but not loving. "Why didn't you love me, Lynda?"

"Kyle—" Her voice broke and immediately he scooped her up, carrying her through to the bedroom.

Bringing herself back to reality was beyond her. Nothing made any sense at all, and she was too far gone to unravel his complexities. Her body had a compulsive will of its own—at times too powerful to obey any directive from the brain.

Later she would recall the intolerability of sharing Kyle with another woman. Later she would feel the pain of the wound too deep for healing.

He could take her whenever he wanted, and he knew it. Kyle wanted her now, and he had won.

No Alternative

Margaret Way

Harlequin Books

TORONTO • NEW YORK • LONDON
AMSTERDAM • PARIS • SYDNEY • HAMBURG
STOCKHOLM • ATHENS • TOKYO • MILAN

Original hardcover edition published in 1983
by Mills & Boon Limited

ISBN 0-373-02639-0

Harlequin Romance first edition August 1984

CHAPTER ONE

THE day began with an argument, and Lynda took her coffee and walked out on to the verandah, staring out distractedly at the overgrown garden. Ten days away and the place was a jungle. She would have to ring and get a man in to lop the trees. Their growth over the past few months of the rainy season had been phenomenal even for the sub-tropics. The great poincianas, their brilliant Christmas blooming over, spread massive acid and emerald green fronds to the ground, their interlocking branches all but blocking out their view of the river, and the New Zealand pohutakawa their mother had planted was threatening to lift their picturesque early Queenslander right off its timber stumps. Of course it should never have been planted so close to the house, but no one had really envisaged such a giant, any more than they had envisaged the pending drama of their lives.

Lynda's fingers came up automatically to pinch back the rampant allamanda. It climbed the white timber columns that supported the overhanging roof and cascaded down the panels of white wrought-iron lace. The glossy leaves and showy yellow trumpets were heavy with rain and she gave a little sagging movement forward of helplessness. There were too many things to do; too many decisions, too many disappointments and heartbreaks. Now, more than ever, she felt like a pawn.

The rain came down again and she jerked her head back impatiently. The river was at flood tide, not the silvery-grey expanse they were used to, but Yangtse mud. Like everyone else whose house fronted on to the river, Lynda had been praying for the rains to soon be over. With its river and numerous creeks, Brisbane was prone to widespread and disruptive flooding during the wet season. If the rains did not stop, there could be a crisis—a natural one to match the manmade one she could see was coming. As a schoolgirl she had lived through the great flood of '74 when the torrential rains that followed cyclone Wanda had caused the river to rise alarmingly. Their house had gone under water, as indeed did every house in the tree-lined street. There was a price to be paid for having the river at the bottom of one's garden, but terrible as the ordeal had been, no one had thought to move. The river remained, broad and deep and luminous . . . but they all continued to watch it.

When Martin came out to her she made no effort to turn to speak to him, and he came to her side, his thin tanned hands gripping the banister.

'I'm sorry, Lyn,' he said tremulously, like a teenager instead of a brilliant young accountant with a first-class Economics degree.

'I'm sorry too. Kyle is the last person in the world I ever wanted you to work for.'

'But he offered me such a challenge, Lyn!' Martin's thin hand came up to clasp her shoulder. 'He doesn't speak about you at all.'

'I don't *ever* want to meet him.'

'Do give me credit for respecting your feelings.'

'That's funny.' Lynda dipped her cloudy dark head, averting her face so her brother couldn't see the sparkle of tears in her eyes. 'Of all the people in the world you had to go and work for my ex-husband!'

'You should never have broken up,' Martin said

violently. 'I never saw two people in my life more in love than you and Kyle. God, he could never take his eyes off you, and he had the face of a god for you.'

'Yes, I didn't see the clay feet.'

'Don't be bitter, Lyn,' he urged.

'I'm not bitter,' she shrugged. 'I've made a new life for myself, Martin, and I never want to meet Kyle again. Don't ever bring him here.'

'Of course not!' Martin protested. 'As though he would want to come here anyway. He's cut you out of his life as ruthlessly as you left him.'

'I didn't *leave* him,' Lynda burst out emotionally, 'I had to go. It was the hardest thing I've ever had to do in my life, and now it's over.'

'I'm sorry, Lyn,' Martin spoke quietly, without inflection, 'but I can't see any better organisation to work for than Endco. It ranks with the biggest blue chip stocks in the country. Kyle is brilliant. He has a wonderful financial career in front of him. For all Sir Neville's sons and grandsons, Kyle is the chosen one. No one thought anyone could improve on the Old Man until Kyle started to show them these past few years. The Endfields would have to be one of the wealthiest families in a very wealthy State.'

'All the more reason why you should separate yourself from Kyle's side,' said Lynda bitterly. 'I have the feeling he might destroy you.'

'Oh, come, come, Lyn,' Martin groaned. 'Must you be so dramatic?'

'Look what happened to me.' Her smoky eyes were wide and troubled. 'We're just ordinary people, Martin. There is no way we can hope to enter the Endfield world without getting hurt. You're even getting yourself into serious debt trying to keep up with Joel.'

'Damn it all, Lynda, I'm not!'

'You are. Kyle is one thing, another Sir Neville, but Joel is little more than a playboy. And he's a very bad influence on you. I couldn't be more unhappy.'

'So you've said over and over.' Martin pounded the banister with such force he hurt the side of his hand. 'Am I supposed to turn aside success because you were once married to Kyle Endfield?'

'You were doing quite well with Campbells.'

'Hell, Lyn,' he said angrily, 'Kyle doubled my salary almost at once. Even getting a place in the firm flattered me out of my mind. They only employ the best!'

'You're clever, Martin, I know that.' The whole world was grey, like her mood.

'Do you realise I've had two promotions in six months?' he demanded.

'You're becoming more and more Kyle's man,' Lyn jeered.

'I have the greatest respect for him, Lyn.' Martin summed up his feelings in a few words. 'I can't condemn him because your marriage didn't work out. He was always great to me. It's hard to realise he's only six years older than I am. He has so much . . . consequence.'

'Oh, Martin!' It was a helpless, empty gesture. She couldn't deny it. There had always been about Kyle an aura of real power which, in combination with his striking good looks, drew men as well as women to him. When Kyle walked into a room, no matter how crowded, everyone looked up. He had it, the charisma. Had it, used it. He had used it on her.

'I guess we all make mistakes,' Martin was saying. 'I could have sworn when you left him, you cut him to the heart. I don't know what you expected of him, Lyn.'

'You're taking his part?'

'You never did explain. I always thought the Endfields with their money and sophistication were too much for you.'

'So they were,' she said harshly. 'One doesn't have a great deal of confidence at nineteen, just a sense of self-preservation. His family didn't want me. Only Lady Endfield was kind. Now she's gone. I don't regret it. Our bitterest experiences are the best teachers of all. The Endfields take what they want, properties, companies, people and when they finish with them, they're unrecognisable. That wasn't going to happen to me. I could never condone or be part of Kyle's life. He was, *is*, totally committed to power, a man of ruthless ambition.'

Martin shook his head, not the least convinced. 'You didn't think like that when you married him, and I don't think like that now. Kyle has another side to him beside the brilliant tycoon. He cares about people and the human condition. When there was that cave-in at Curnock and two men were trapped down the mine didn't he fly there immediately and go down himself with the Chief Engineer?'

'It's their mine.' Lynda looked straight ahead into the rain.

'He didn't have to go down, Lyn,' Martin pointed out quietly. 'And he did get them out.'

'I never said he lacked courage.'

'He's very popular with the men,' he persisted. 'They all come up and speak to him when they'd find that impossible with the Old Man. He's so gruff and intolerant. He must have more enemies than friends.'

'But then he prefers to be feared than loved.' Lynda dismissed Sir Neville Endfield severely. In marrying her Kyle had defied his grandfather, but it had only taken a little over two years for Kyle to discard her.

'Will this rain never stop?' Martin was desperate to change the subject. He loved his sister, but he had come to realise he coveted a lot of things she didn't, things he could never attain in the ordinary course of events. Lynda with her beauty, her intelligence and grace of manner had won for herself the most eligible man imaginable and for whatever reason had let him get away. Martin did not intend ever to fall out with his ex-brother-in-law. All their lives had been fatally entwined, and although Kyle was a rich and exceptionally attractive man he had never remarried. He wasn't a man to make a mistake, and he had made his greatest one with Lynda.

'We'll have to have the trees lopped,' Lynda sighed. 'Just look at them! I've never seen anything like their growth over the past months. The whole place is a wilderness. With so much vegetation we risk having a snake in the house. I've seen a large one on the lower terrace since I've been home.'

'Oh, snakes!' Martin dismissed them nonchalantly. 'We've lived with them all our lives, so close to the water.'

'I still don't fancy one as a bedmate.' Lynda moved back and sat down in the planter's chair. 'You'll have to give me a hand at the weekend, Martin.'

'I will.' Martin moved uncomfortably. 'What you really should do is sell. People will pay anything for these old Queensland colonials. And when you're on the river you can nearly name your own price.'

'I'm not selling,' she said quietly, more than ever grateful their father had left the house to her.

'Then don't whinge about not getting any board,' Martin said with immense resentment. 'Dad left the house to you, which was pretty unfair. I'm never home for my meals, in any case.'

'Oh, you manage to have a few.' Lynda pushed her own resentments out of her mind. What was the use of talking about electricity and rates and maintenance? She had no wish to evict her brother, though she often thought it extraordinary that he made no attempt to find a bachelor pad of his own. The thing was, he needed every cent of his high salary to maintain a lifestyle acceptable to the likes of Kyle's younger brother, Joel. 'Please don't let's talk any more. I have a headache.'

'Apparently you don't care if *I* have one,' Martin accused her. 'Why do you always have to interfere? I can manage my own life.'

Despite her intention to stay quiet Lynda found herself gritting her teeth. 'The Porsche was a mistake. You're not in that league yet—and you have so many clothes you can't even get to wear them. Now you've allowed Joel to introduce you to gambling. What does it matter to him if he loses a hundred dollars, a thousand, ten thousand for that matter? I saw the other day where the family sold their coal lease at Burranjong for five million dollars.'

'Five and a half million,' Martin objected.

'How can you possible complete with that?' Lynda said wearily. 'And anyway, who would want to?'

'I sure as hell would!' Martin cried enthusiastically. 'I want to be a big success, Lyn. Can't you understand that?'

'Well, Martin, you can be. There's plenty of scope for us all, but it's extremely unlikely, for instance, that you're going to challenge the Endfield dynasty.'

'I'm not challenging them at all. I've joined them.'

'I can't be happy about it.' Lynda's long black

lashes veiled her smoky eyes. 'Joel isn't Kyle. He's shallow and vain and when it suits him a most accomplished liar.'

'He always asks after you,' Martin countered. 'It's not all smooth sailing for Joel either. He couldn't be Kyle if he tried, and everyone seems to blame him for it except his mother.'

'Quite frankly, I think he's earned his grandfather's poor opinion,' said, Lynda. 'He never tried to do anything in his life except spend money and have a good time.'

'Half his luck!.

'You don't mean that, Martin,' Lynda said sadly. 'There has to be a purpose in life, some sense of accomplishment. Something to offer the people we love. Joel is the living proof that money is not enough.'

'You're so serious-minded, Lyn,' Martin told her.

'One does need to be serious-minded sometimes.'

Martin grunted. 'Just the same, you act more like thirty-four than twenty-four. What's the big deal about a bit of harmless fun?.

Lynda rubbed the tips of her fingers over her aching forehead. 'I can see the strain in you, Martin. You're not the same person you were six months ago. I've tried to explain what trying to keep pace with the Endfields is doing to you. You must put it out of your mind. Next time Joel mentions going off to the races tell him you're going wind-surfing instead.'

'I'm off wind-surfing,' said Martin.

'You're off everything you used to love. I don't hear any more about the boat you and Perry were going to build. Come to that, Perry only calls in now and again. He used to be your very best friend.'

'He was starting to get on my nerves a bit.'

'Like me,' said Lynda. 'Perry wouldn't hesitate to speak his mind.'

'He's a good bloke in his way,' Martin admitted, 'but he'll never get anywhere.'

'There are differing opinions about what constitutes "getting somewhere". Perry might not be interested in becoming a millionaire, but I'm pretty certain he'll never get into debt. His real concern in life is to function to the best of his ability and not set his sights impossibly high.'

'Meaning *I* do?.

Lynda looked up at her brother long and searchingly.

'You're a climber, Martin, we both know that.'

'It's a pity *you* weren't,' Martin laughed bitterly, pleased with his quick retort.

'I married Kyle because I loved him.'

'You weren't attracted by all that money?'

'In a way it repelled me,' she told him.

'Then you're a freak!' Martin regarded her with derision.

'I'm sorry you're not a bit more like me.' Lynda suddenly looked very fragile. 'If you allow yourself to get into trouble you'll find Kyle Endfield relentless. He could even be testing you now. There is no way you'll get to the top with Endco unless you put Joel and the social whirl completely to one side. Think about it. No sacrifice is too great for Kyle. It didn't just happen he's a superpower because his grandfather is Sir Neville Endfield. Everything in him, his brain, his burning energy, his physical strength and his will power, is all brought together so that his grandfather's ideas and now his own are brought to reality. One day Kyle *will* be Endco.'

'Yes, he will,' Martin agreed, visibly brightening.

'If I didn't admire him so much I'd be crazy with envy.'

'Then you can't possibly know the hard work that goes on after the office is closed. For tycoons, Martin, it's pretty nearly a twenty-four-hour day. I know—I remember.'

'And you wanted out,' Martin pointed out dryly.

'It was a question of survival.' Lynda's smoky eyes looked almost translucent. 'You can't possibly know what it was like.'

'And you've never told anyone.' Martin gave her a hard, accusatory look. 'Except maybe Scott Walker. Now there's one safe, steady, one hundred per cent decent guy.'

'Why bring Scott into this?' Lynda asked.

'Why not? He seems to be assuming some importance in your life.'

'You sound disapproving,' she commented.

'He's too old for you, Lyn. And too tame.'

'Well, I was married to a brilliant dynamo, and look where it got me.'

'Maybe you were too young or something,' Martin said hesitantly. 'Things would have been different, I'm sure, if we hadn't lost Mum and Dad. One terrible accident and our whole lives were changed. I don't think anyone will ever get me to go up in a light aircraft.'

'Yet Sir Neville has his own jet and three or four Gulfstream Commanders on standby,' Lynda reminded him.

'That's the normal form of business transport in a State two and half times the size of Texas.'

'So one day you can expect to fly in one.'

'Ah, well, I guess we can't fight destiny anyway.' His voice betrayed their never-ending sense of loss.

'Why did it happen, Lyn?'

'One day we might know the answers.' She looked at him, feeling the same overwhelming sense of unreality. Their parents had set off on a tour of the Outback, an adventure which was to have lasted three or four months. A week later, one early morning the light aircraft they had decided to charter was found in a dried-up creek bed on Reverley station. The pilot had been young with not a great deal of experience, and they had all died together and shared a column in the newspaper. There were times when Lynda still woke up sweating and deeply distressed from her recurrent nightmare. Maybe her marriage wouldn't have failed had she had her parents to turn to for advice. Maybe Martin would see the truth of what he was doing to himself now, with their father to point it out. She was only offending him and making him angry, whereas their father had always had a way of making them calmly face a situation. Martin would have listened to their father, only Lynda knew she wouldn't be able to stop him from overreaching himself in dangerous competition with Joel Endfield and his rich friends.

She sighed deeply and stood up, a small girl, delicately made. At eighteen, a single day before their parents had been killed, she had been wonderfully pretty, her silky dark curls cut short, her large, very beautiful smoky eyes always filled with light and a happy expression. At twenty-four she was beautiful, refined in every way, but the gaiety was gone. She would have made a very striking model for a painter who wished to portray a sensitive young woman who had suffered too much for love.

'Shall I drop you off at the office?' Martin asked.

'Yes, please.' It was necessary to get dressed and continue with life. 'Will you be home this evening?'

'Sort of. About eight.'
Lynda moved inside.

Soon after the break-up of her marriage Lynda went
back to work, assuring the Endfield lawyers that she
would not touch a cent of the massive settlement Kyle
had wished to force on her.

'But my dear girl, you *ought* to,' her own solicitor
had told her, but Lynda's decision had been
vehemently expressed and final. She wanted nothing
from her ex-husband, not even his name; a positively
unusual decision that had made the legal world reel. To
refuse a fortune! But that, Lynda with her nature
found easy. It was the pain, she knew, that would be
with her for ever.

At first she wanted to go away, but there was
Martin and the house and the consideration that she
had been offered a job with Prescott & Walker, a
highly reputable firm of chartered accountants. Her
understandable fear was she would run into Kyle on
the steps of a building or even at some function, and
she knew the sight of him, the sound of his voice,
would twist the knife deeply in a wound that would
never heal. Then, as the weeks went on, driven by
Martin's apparent need of her she had asked Scott
Walker to take her on, never grasping that he had been
deeply attracted to her the very first time they had
met. It had been an art showing and although Scott
Walker could not remember the name of the artist, he
had never forgotten Mrs Kyle Endfield's young,
haunting beauty. He told himself afterwards it was a
sense of friendship, responsibility, that made him offer
her a job, but he knew in his heart it was really so he
could look at her. At first she worked as receptionist,
doing a little office work and typing, but she was so

quick and intelligent and so swiftly proficient at secretarial skills she replaced one of the firm's retiring secretaries and eventually moved up to become Scott Walker's own private and confidential secretary, with access to a lot of information about important people and their businesses. It would not have been true to say Lynda enjoyed her job. It was neither a pleasure nor simply a means of efficiently filling in her time. It was more that she felt her life was empty; that nothing unbearably beautiful or tender or passionate would happen to her any more. She had loved Kyle with every atom of her being and he had taken so much away from her, all she was left with was a desperate kind of pride.

Scott was waiting for her when she arrived at the office, a severely fastidious, rather handsome man in his early forties.

'Lynda.' His pleasant, educated voice lifted with pleasure. 'One gets so tired of the rain!'

'Of course,' she smiled at him, 'Queenslanders can't accept anything less than our almost perpetual blue skies.'

'Yes, we do have a splendid climate. Mustn't forget that. 'He went on looking for a file amidst the papers on his desk, and Lynda, with supreme confidence and the uncanny intuitive skills she had developed, found it for him in half the time.

'Is this what you're looking for?' she asked.

'I can't get used to you, Lynda.' Suddenly he laughed. 'That's it, Hartley-McNab. Might as well get it over. A few years ago they were nobody at all, now since they got that contract from . . .'

'Endco,' Lynda's voice was sweet and blank.

'Why, if nothing changes they'll finish up millionaires.'

'Will you be wanting me for the next hour?' Lynda asked.

'No.' Scott lifted his head, the expression in his eyes changing from businesslike and slightly amused to curiously defenceless and humble. 'I'm expected at that reception for Sir Philip Gascombe on Friday evening. Could I beg you to come?'

'What time is it, Scott?' She was obeying an inbuilt directive not to hurt him.

'Oh, six to eight, the usual thing at the Convention Room at the Cultural Centre. Afterwards. I thought we might have dinner.'

He wanted her to so badly Lynda felt his tension coming at her in waves. 'That would be lovely, Scott. I'll wear something simple I can dress up.'

'You couldn't fail to look lovely no matter what you wore.'

He was in love with her, she knew that, and in the end she might come to care for him. No passion. No pain. Only gentle affection, an ease together, an end to her limbo, with comfort in a man's touch.

By late Thursday afternoon everyone knew the rains were over and a brilliant sun shone out of a peacock sky.

'I'll be driving down to the Coast for the weekend,' Martin told Lynda in the few moments before he set her down in the city on Friday morning.

'Oh, Martin, I was hoping you'd help me in the garden. It's terribly overgrown.'

'Surely it will be too wet?' Martin felt bound to excuse himself.

'Not at all. It will dry out swiftly with this sun on it.'

'I can't stay here, sweetie,' Martin indicated the loading zone. 'See you Sunday night.'

'Who are you going with, Martin?' she asked him, certain in her heart it would be Joel.

'Don't worry,' he waved his finger at her chidingly. 'I won't come to any harm.'

Of course it would be Joel, and maybe a small house party comprising at least two beautiful girls.

It was a hectic day, with Scott closeted with two of his most important and therefore demanding clients, and at the end of it Lynda felt like tottering home instead of going on to a function.

'Well, what do you think?' she asked Susan, one of the other secretaries, who was eyeing her appreciatively.

'Very, very nice.'

'Like my shoes?'

'Beautiful.' Susan looked down at the elegant silver sandals that matched Lynda's over-the-shoulder evening bag. Her dress was a matt white jersey, a twenties style with a dropped waistline that sat neatly on her narrow hips, and she had changed the earrings she had worn all day for silver pendants set with moonstones that seemed to do fantastic things to her eyes. With the earrings went two silver bracelets and to Susan's admiring eyes she looked the essence of luxury, and all on a working girl's budget.

'You know,' Susan said said wisely, 'Scotty's a nice guy and he could afford to keep a girl in some style, but you're meant for altogether different things.'

'Such as?' Lynda no longer flinched at such observations. Although they were friendly and often had lunch together Lynda had never mentioned her private life; not the fact that she had once been married, let alone to a man as well known as Kyle Endfield. She wore no rings and she used her maiden name. So far as Susan was concerned, they were both seeking husbands together.

'Oh, well, someone *exciting*!' Susan's blue eyes

positively glittered. 'You've got a certain look about you. Classy. You need someone who can trundle you into a little ol' Rolls. Not Scotty's Volvo.'

'If anything, I prefer the Volvo,' said Lynda.

'You must be crazy!' Susan shook her blonde head in wonderment. 'In any case, you've never been in a Rolls.'

Oh, I have. Many times. Lynda's smiling expression altered entirely so that Susan burst out in surprise.

'What's the matter with you?'

'How do you mean?' Lynda turned back to the mirror, pretending to pay attention to the dark, cloudy aureole of her hair.

'You looked so strange—so sad and, what's the word . . . introspective. Gary Taylor says you're a girl with secrets.'

'And he's wasted a great deal of his time trying to chat me up.'

'I'm sure he has,' Susan moaned. 'Gary is rather nice. Do you mind if I have him?'

'Play hard to get,' Lynda advised.

'Gosh,' said Susan, 'I wish *I* was a femme fatale!'

When they arrived at the function the large room was already crowded and people were spilling out on to the terraces that overlooked the river.

'A drink, sir, madam?' a waiter muttered, and was gone.

'Good grief, what a crush!' Scott took a grateful sip of champagne. 'Let's go out on to the terrace, shall we? The breeze off the river is glorious.'

They wandered off, stopping here and there a dozen times to exchange a few pleasantries with acquaintances. Anyone who was anyone in the professional and political life of the city seemed to be there, plus a fair sprinkling of socialites, and Lynda began to feel it would have been better to hurt Scott's feelings and stay home instead. Indeed, as the evening progressed she found she couldn't subdue a prickling along her nerves that persisted to the point when her heart began to beat faster to sheer agitation. A full-page article in the morning papers less than a week ago had informed her that Sir Neville was in Japan for a series of business discussions, and these days wherever Sir Neville went, his favourite grandson and heir apparent was sure to go.

She stared at the distinguished speaker who introduced the guest of honour with a short but glowing accounts of his high achievements, but in reality never heard a word.

'Old fraud,' Scott whispered in her ear. 'He once took libel action against him.'

After the speeches, the waiters circled again, and as Lynda turned to set down her delicate wine flute she was brought up so catastrophically the wine glass fell out of her nerveless hand and shattered on the polished floor.

'Don't worry about it,' said Scott, talking rapidly, but then he stopped. Lynda had turned so alarmingly pale he was terrified she was about to faint. 'My dear!' he put an arm about her. In the heat of a summer evening, she felt cold.

'No worries, sir,' a waiter was saying, scooping glittering fragments deftly into a dust pan. 'There, it's gone.'

Scanning heads had turned to see what was the trouble, then decided a broken wine glass was scarcely worth the trouble. Lynda, however, still stood like a statue.

'So people are breaking glasses all the time,' Scott murmured kindly.

The small graven statue stirred. 'May we go, Scott?'

Even her voice sounded lifeless.

'But of course!' Scott looked up, seeking the nearest exit, and as he did so he saw that a man had entered the vast convention room, halfway arrested as Lynda had been, his startling blue eyes on them, his striking face hard and cold.

Kyle Endfield.

He had not expected to see him any more than Lynda, who had once been owned by the man.

The sight of him was torture. Lynda wanted to move, but a paralysis had taken possession of her limbs. Kyle ... *Kyle*. For long moments she was naked and vulnerable, remembering the touch of his body on hers, the imprint of his mouth. She was starving for him, and her heart's unbidden admission made her reaction all the more violent.

'Please, Scott, I must go,' she muttered.

'I know you must.' He took her slender, breakable arm tightly. 'Keep calm, my dear. I'll get you out of here.'

What would people think? She was drunk? Ill? Ill, most likely. People seemed very sincere in their efforts to make a clear path for them. Lynda did not, *could* not look again in her ex-husband's direction, but he continued to watch them as they made their way through the crowd.

'Fascinating—did you see that?' One society lady asked another. 'That was the girl Kyle Endfield married.'

'Of course, it would be. Both of them seemed turned to stone.'

'Want to meet him?' the first lady asked.

'I certainly do. He's gorgeous!'

Even seated in Scott's car Lynda still couldn't control the wild beating of her heart.

'I'm so sorry, Scott,' she apologised.

'But you do see him at different times, don't you?' Scott asked.

Lynda couldn't control the shudder than ran over her body. 'I haven't laid eyes on him since the divorce.'

'But that seems impossible,' Scott protested. 'I mean, even a large city is a small place when all the top people know one another.'

'I'm not a top person. Scott,' she said in a stressful-sounding voice. 'I never was. It seems a nightmare that I was ever married to Kyle at all.'

'He looked as if he could strangle you,' Scott muttered, still feeling the violent affront.

'No, he's just never forgiven me for messing up his life even briefly.'

Scott looked down into her delicate, oval face. Her head was thrown back and he thought, not for the first time, that sometimes she looked too fragile to withstand the slightest brutality. Unquestionably the sight of her ex-husband had upset her dreadfully.

'I know you won't feel like dinner, but won't you come home with me? I want to look after you, Lynda. You must know that.' His hand moved to her hair. It was very silky and naturally curly, expertly cut so it waved away from her flawless-skinned face, its upturned whorls just clearing her shoulders. He wanted to kiss her so badly it was an ache in him, but he realised anxiously that she was in a state of shock. 'Please come,' he said softly. 'We can talk. It might even help you to let things out.'

She didn't answer, and for the first time he took the initiative into his own hands. In any case he couldn't possibly permit her to go home to an empty house to brood. That brother of hers, though a very attractive and likeable young man, one wished was a stronger

character and more considerate of his sister. A very
curious thing that he had gone to work for Endco. One
might wish to know his motive—and more pertinently,
Kyle Endfield's motive for taking him on.

Scott still lived in the house that had been in his
family for three generations, and Lynda experienced a
sense of peace as soon as she stepped inside the front
door.

'I've often wanted to bring you here,' Scott told her.
'Sit down, my dear. On the sofa, or armchair.' He
took her evening bag from her and put it down on a
beautiful little inlaid table.

'You must be hungry, Scott?' She knew quite well
he hadn't stopped for lunch.

'So, we'll get something later.' He sat down
opposite her, a cool man who looked well with
formality. 'Won't it help to share your troubles?'

'I didn't come here, Scott, to burden you with any
discussion,' she sighed.

'But then you've never discussed your marriage,
have you?'

'No, never.' Her soft, melodic voice was metallic.
'It's too personal—too private.'

'Keeping it all in might destroy you.' Her beautiful
skin, lightly gilded from the summer sun, still had a
pronounced pallor.

'I know it.' Her body couldn't relax.

'So can't you trust me?.' he asked simply, and if she
had been looking at him she would have seen the
devotion in his normally impassive eyes.

'There's really nothing to tell, Scott.' She did look
up at him then. 'I got married very early with my
whole heart, whole mind, whole body—and that's my
trouble. I'll never be whole anymore. Sometimes it
scares me.'

'So what happened?' Scott asked, perplexed. 'I saw Endfield's face tonight and like you he still has an enormous residue of feeling. So what went wrong?'

'I couldn't cope.' She sank small white teeth in her softly moulded lower lip. 'Too many in-laws, too much jealousy and interference. I was too young, obviously, too inexperienced to hold Kyle.'

'But I've heard that *you* left *him*?' Scott shrugged his shoulders apologetically. 'You know how people talk.'

'I did leave him, Scott,' said Lynda in a very low voice. 'I couldn't accept the Endfield way of life.' I couldn't accept that Kyle could lie with another woman. But wild horses wouldn't drag *that* disclosure out of her.

'So it was over just like that?' Scott's well-bred face looked somewhat stupefied. 'Couldn't you have worked out your differences?'

And condone something unforgivable? 'No, we couldn't,' she said briefly. 'His family were shocked when he told them he was going to marry me.'

'Whatever for?' Scott reacted instantly to the anguish. 'You're a beautiful girl, sensitive, intelligent—you have everything.'

'Apparently it wasn't enough. You know Olivia Schofield?'

'Who doesn't?' Scott said a little scornfully. 'Rich bitch. I've been introduced to her several times, but she always manages to look through me.'

'I can appreciate that,' Lynda said wryly. 'Olivia did everything in her power to prove to me that I didn't fit. And she was right. Sometimes I feel a little bitter, but it's no consolation to know Kyle didn't marry her even when he was free of me. She was the family choice.'

'Do you actually mean that?' Scott looked surprised.

'Surely you'd heard?'

'Then why hasn't he married her?'

'Probably he's woken up to the fact that she's not a very nice girl, but at one time they were supposed to be very serious about one another. Certainly she was a great favourite of Kyle's mother and sister. They got along beautifully—all committed to the good life.'

'That's obvious,' Scott said dryly. 'A small percentage of the family are high achievers and the rest do absolutely nothing and get away with it.'

'They have nothing to work *for*,' Lynda explained a little awkwardly. 'In theory it sounds marvellous to be rich, but somehow a lot of rich people lose their way— the ones that aren't actually concerned with preserving the family fortunes, Christine, Kyle's sister, hasn't done a tap of work since the day she was born, and his brother Joel . . .'

'Is just as big as playboy as he could be,' Scott interrupted disapprovingly. 'Why Martin chooses to run around with him, I don't know.'

Lynda looked at him with surprise. 'Whatever do you mean?'

'Oh, come now, my dear,' Scott said without a second's hesitation, 'I know you have your problems with Martin.'

'I have no problem with Martin,' Lynda maintained, growing faintly angry.

'I want to *help* you, Lynda,' Scott said anxiously. 'but you won't let anyone get close to you. Look, I'm not going to dictate to you about your own brother, but I'm not a fool, and I happen to care about you. I know Martin doesn't give you anywhere near the support you deserve, and I have the suspicion lately he's causing you a good deal of heartache.'

'Never.' Lynda shook her head.

'Okay, you say never, but I know you too well. You're deeply worried, and I don't blame you. It was the greatest mistake for Martin to leave his old job.'

'When all's said and done he's on twice the salary,' she pointed out reasonably.

'And spending the whole lot, I'm sure,' 'Scott said fervently. 'I'm in a very much better position, but let me tell you *I* couldn't afford his car.'

'Just a young man showing off,' Lynda shrugged.

'I know that well,' Scott shifted his position to hold Lynda's hand, 'but the point is if he tries to stay the pace of Joel Endfield's circle he's bound to run into trouble. I'm not a disinterested bystander here, I'm very fond of you, Lynda. Have you any idea?'

She was genuinely appalled by the thought of involvement. She liked and trusted Scott very much, but she couldn't even contemplate him as a lover. Kyle had cured her of all that.

'You're very good to me, Scott,' she offered gently.

'You're special.' He could feel her withdrawal. 'Now, I wonder how we can steer Martin away from Endfields? One would almost have thought your ex-husband did this deliberately. I suppose it would suit him nicely to have Martin in the firm. It would make it easier for him to keep a check on you.'

'I'm sure that wasn't the plan,' Lynda said sceptically. 'Kyle wrote me off a long time ago.'

'Then I wonder why he looked murder tonight?'

'He didn't care to confront me any more than I could bear to confront him.'

'God, what a terrible thing!' Scott exclaimed. 'He must have loved you a great deal. I mean, you said yourself he went against his family, and that would have taken some doing.'

'You don't know Kyle,' Lynda said wearily, her face like carved ivory. 'He's unstoppable when it comes to something he wants.'

'And he wanted *you*.'

'For a while.'

'I can't accept that,' Scott said curiously. 'I can't imagine any man wanting to let you go—and don't forget I saw his face tonight. I think if we'd been any closer he might have broken you in two. Me as well.'

'So he was livid?' Lynda rose to her feet. 'Show me the kitchen, Scott. I'm going to get you something to eat.'

'God only knows that's there.'

'Eggs?'

'Yes, I think so. Anyway, I do know there's a bottle of champagne.'

In the end, with what little there was in Scott's bachelor refrigerator Lynda made them puffy bacon omelettes which she dressed up with a cheese sauce and followed it up with a fresh green salad because Scott had run out of everything but lettuce, a cucumber, two sticks of celery, half a green pepper and some shallots.

'Delicious!' he said, and he certainly looked sincere. 'Here's to you and me!' He lifted his wineglass.

'Why have you never married, Scott,' Lynda asked carefully. 'You're such a nice man.'

'I've had to wait to find someone to love.' For one long moment he searched her smoky eyes. 'Dare I hope you could ever come to care for me?'

'Oh, Scott!' An ache started to twist in her breast. She would never be able to love again.

'Eat your omelette,' Soctt said firmly. 'You look so fragile a puff of wind could blow you away.' Scott wasn't a fool and he knew he had said enough.

Whatever had happened to Lynda during her brief, disastrous marriage, she wasn't over it yet. Quietly and casually he began to talk about other things.

CHAPTER TWO

LYNDA's thoughts turned to Martin many times the next day, as she was marketing in the morning at a busy shopping centre and later in the afternoon. It was one thing to pursue one's ambitions all week and quite another to ignore one's home duties at the weekend.

It was brilliantly fine. Perfect weather for the beach, she was forced to concede, but there were so many jobs that needed to be done—small repairs around the house. She looked up at the plastered ceiling numbly. The rain had come through and spoilt the paintwork, which meant there was a leak somewhere in the roof. She would have to pay a man to get up there. Martin certainly wouldn't, although as a boy he had climbed over every inch searching out lost tennis balls in the guttering. What had happened to Martin? When had it started? The rational part of her knew Martin's self-absorption had not begun when Kyle offered him a job. He had been changing probably from the time of the tragedy. She could do no more than she was doing to help him, yet he was more and more loath to help her.

The garden almost defeated her. It was a riot of brilliant colour and heavy with summer scents, but even the kindest person would have called it a flowering wilderness. The quote she had received for lopping the trees had seemed to her exorbitant, so she decided to saw off all the branches she could reach herself. It would be too humiliating to have to start up the motor mower, but she supposed she would have to. The rain had even brought up scores of mushrooms so that the farthest reach of the large garden looked like a farm. Really she should take a photograph, the mushrooms looked so funny—an army of them, marching in their ranks along the great banks of hydrangeas. She had no idea if one could eat them or not, but somehow they looked magical.

Of course the motor mower wouldn't start, or she was too weak to give it the necessary pull. Would there ever be time in Martin's life to do the things a man was supposed to do? It even occured to her that she was ruining him for some poor girl. He would be utterly useless.

'Hey, Lynda!' a young voice called to her. 'Let me do that.'

She looked back and straightened, a welcoming smile lightening her rather strained face.

'Hi, Darren. No cricket this afternoon?'

'We played this morning.'

'Win?'

'*Of* course.' Darren grinned at her, an engaging fourteen-year-old neighbour with lots of freckles and the most beautiful red-gold hair. 'Tennis this afternoon, but not until three o'clock. We couldn't get the court until then.' He went to the motor mower, told Lynda to hold it steady, then pulled the cord exactly once. The motor fired at once with a choking puff of smoke and Darren immediately made some adjustments.

'Where's Martin?' he shouted.

'Down on the beach.'

'Why aren't you?'

'I wasn't invited.'

'I want to know why Martin always lets you clean up the yard?' the boy said, his amber eyes strangely

filled with hostility. 'I mean, he's six feet tall, and
you're only a little slip of a thing shorter than me.'

'Oh, he's busy, Darren,' Lynda protested.

'I'll do the back first,' said Darren, 'then I'll run
around the front. This is much too hard work for you.'

There was no sense in getting angry. Martin was
getting a lot of people fired up lately and she had
known Darren's parents all her life. They were very
nice, kindly people, and she was aware of their
exasperation with Martin even if Darren had been the
only one to put their disapproval into words. Only a
month ago Darren and his father had come in to cut
back the bougainvillea, which though dazzling in its
brilliant array was such a rampant grower it had to be
pruned heavily to be contained. Martin had told her *he*
wasn't going to be torn to pieces by the vicious thorns.
Martin was very particular about his appearance.

Back in house Lynda assembled iced lemonade for
Darren for when he was finished and cut him two
slices of the chocolate cake she had brought for
Martin. It had been expensive, but she knew from
experience it was as luscious as it looked.

'Gee, that's beaut!' said Darren, happily munching
later. 'Did you make it?'

'No, bought it this time. Thanks a lot, Darren.
You're a pal.'

'And you're a good pal to me!' Darren maintained
stoutly, not in the least embarrassed to have Lynda
patting him on the shoulder. 'Who types out all my
special assignments?'

She smiled at him. 'I learn a lot.'

'Mum thinks you're the best girl in the whole world.
It's rotten, what's happened to you. Really *rotten*. You
know, I thought that husband of yours was really
O.K.'

'I admired him, too, Darren.' Idolised him, God help me!

'Mum was always going on about what a terrific guy he was. She was so happy for you when you got married. Dad liked him too. We all thought he was your knight in shining armour.'

'It wasn't all his fault, Darren.' It was a remarkable discussion, but she realised Darren had always felt close to her, like a young brother.

'It couldn't have been yours, Lyn,' Darren muttered, unimpressed. 'I saw a picture of him the other day in the paper. He looked as if he doesn't smile very often any more.'

'He's older, of course. And he has very many new responsibilities.'

'Remember how he used to smile?' Darren asked, scowling. 'You'd think life would have been simple with you and all that money.'

'Life's never simple, my friend,' Lynda lifted a hand to his thick, curling hair. 'I'm just going to pray *you* find the right woman.'

'Don't, you're giving me the shakes!' Darren protested.

'Perhaps it *wasn't* you I saw pedalling after Alana Norris?'

Darren blushed. 'She's older than I am anyway.'

'Never mind. You're a whole lot taller.'

They parted amicably and Lynda turned her attention to scooping the leaves off the swimming pool. The filter needed cleaning out, but it was heavy to lift. How frustrating it was sometimes to be female. Even fourteen-year-old Darren far exceeded her physical strength. The Kreepy-Krauly wouldn't go unless she cleaned out that filter. Just for a moment she thought she would be perfectly happy to drown, only she was an excellent swimmer, raised like a water baby.

By late afternoon she was breathless with exertion, but with the lawn neatly mown and and all the lower branches of the poincianas down the grounds were looking very much tidier. There was a speedboat out on the river pulling a girl on water skis. She was very good, but no better, Lynda thought mildly, than herself. Once she and Martin had zoomed up and down the river. He had even taught her to ride his surfboard, but they never had any fun together any more. They were really very different in temperament as they were in appearance, but for a long time there, while they were growing up, Martin had been the best brother in the world. She could never forget that or reject her feeling of responsibility for him. It was remarkable, though Martin was the elder by two years Lynda had always been the one to get him out of trouble.

'You, my darling,' their father used to say to her, 'are the one with common sense. The lack of it is going to make Martin's life difficult for him.'

She had begun to suspect her father had been right. There was nothing wrong with ambition. Martin wanted to get to the top. Lynda only wished he would concentrate a little more on work and less on play. To Lynda's way of thinking he was out of his mind, to take up with Joel and his crowd the way he had. What good could it possibly do him? Where was all the extra money coming from?

She continued worrying in this vein for some time, deciding she would cool off in the pool after she had dragged the poinciana branches around to the garden shredder. She was wearing a brief, violet-coloured bikini in any case, with a pair of printed shorts pulled on for respectability. Not that anyone could see her except from the river. All the trees and shrubs had grown so high everyone had a private paradise to themselves.

By the time she had all the branches together she had run out of breath, so she had to pause for a few moments to regain it. She felt hot and dishevelled and curiously lightheaded, and one of her slender bare legs had a long angry scratch on it. That would be the pampas grass. She moved into the shade, leaning back against the trunk of the tulip tree waiting for the feeling of lightheadedness to pass. But it was doomed to increase.

As she stood weakly, a man edged his way around the side of the house and she stared at him in overwhelming shock. It *couldn't* be. But he spoke.

'Lynda?' he said curtly.

She found to her horror she was trembling violently. She could not believe it, even as he was moving towards her.

He reached her and those vivid blue eyes, that once used to remind her of sapphires, were brilliant and cold. 'Why look as if you're in the middle of a nightmare? I'm really here.'

'Why?' Her voice didn't come naturally.

'Speak up, Miss Reardon, I can't hear you.'

Anger forced her head up. 'A great many divorced women revert to their maiden names.'

'Of course,' he bowed suavely. 'Especially when they don't value marriage very highly.'

'Why are you here, Kyle?' She lifted a hand to her tousled hair while he stood tall and dangerous, watching her. Indeed he was staring at her so fixedly she felt a slight attack of giddiness.

'Where's Martin?' he asked, his brilliant eyes

flickering, cruel, beautiful eyes under heavy lids.

'Surely you have a better idea than I have?' she asked hoarsely.

'It's important that I speak to him.'

Lynda turned away abruptly, unable to bear his glance on her. 'He's gone away for the weekend, Kyle. He's not here.'

'Is that true?'

'Yes.' With horror she heard the disbelief and contempt in his voice. 'I should say he was with your brother Joel.'

'Did he tell you that?' The curtness in his voice was alarming.

'He didn't tell me anything,' Lynda said forlornly. 'Martin and I don't share a great rapport these days. Not since you took him over.'

'Still worrying yourself silly about Martin?' Kyle moved so he was standing beside her, looking down at her lovely, averted profile.

'Why did you want him, Kyle? Won't you tell me?'

'Why should I tell you anything?' He was obviously forcing himself to speak in a level voice. 'Why should I even waste a moment pitying you for being the strong one in a fragile girl's body? So Martin still doesn't lift a finger to help you?'

'Why do you say that?' She flashed him a brief, shimmering gaze, not angry but poignant.

He was the one who showed the anger, all the more frightening for being tightly controlled. '*Look* at you,' he gritted, and suddenly grasped her hand, forcing up the palm. There was a large blister between her thumb and forefinger from where she had held the hand saw. 'I suppose you cut all those branches down?'

'Because I *like* gardening!' she retorted almost hysterically, the touch of his hand on hers plummetting her into a hateful remembrance of ecstasy.

'How you must hate me,' he said violently. 'If you didn't need me you could have used my money.'

'All I have and all I want is my pride!' she gave the oddest little laugh, jerking her small hand away from him. Could there ever be a hope for tomorrow with a life dominated by yesterday? In the whole world to be only this *one* man? This terrible, dark power?

'Well, you're not nearly as strong and self-sufficient as you'd like to be.' His glittering glance swept the newly mown grounds and although they had been cleaned up to a transforming degree it was still a flaming, tropical wilderness, almost suffocatingly sultry with the brilliant banks of bougainvillea once more on the march and all the flowering fast-growing shrubs as tall and spreading as trees.

'Surely you didn't do the *mowing*?' His glance swung back to her, raking her ethereal frame.

'No, Darren did that.' Her hand was tingling where he had touched it.

'How is he?' Kyle asked unexpectedly.

'Darren?'

'I know how Martin is,' he answered harshly.

'Darren is fine. He's grown very tall.' Only a few hours ago he was talking about you.

'He's a good boy,' Kyle said. 'He'll make a decent man.'

'I expect there are a few,' Lynda shrugged.

'There's one thing—*you* wouldn't know if you met one.'

The tension that was between them was mounting by the moment. 'Martin isn't in any kind of trouble, is he?' she found herself asking.

'There are a few things I'd like him to explain,' he said ironically.

'Such as?' She took a deep, steadying breath.

'Mind your own business, Lynda,' he suggested with alarming gentleness.

'Martin *is* my business.' She forced herself to tilt her head to him. With her flat-sandalled feet he towered over her more than ever.

'Ah, yes, of course,' he drawled. 'Only husbands are marginal figures.'

'You were always jealous of my love for Martin,' she said bitterly.

'My dear girl,' he said, sounding very weary and bored. 'I was always disapproving of your over-protective, little-mother attitude towards a brother a few years your senior.'

'Martin has always needed me,' she said in a low voice. 'I couldn't rid myself of a responsibility because you wanted me to.'

'You've helped to ruin him. Did you know that?' Kyle said brusquely. 'You've never made him lift a finger.'

'Please stop, Kyle,' she begged him. 'You're making me very angry.'

'I wouldn't care if I made you *crazy*,' he said in a taunting voice. 'You're a very odd girl, Lynda. In fact you think quite differently from every other woman I've ever known. What I'm telling you is this. You must take a good deal of the responsibility for never allowing Martin to grow up. The attachment has been too close.'

'We lost our parents!' She felt swept by tears but she wouldn't give way to them.

'I know it all,' he said abruptly. 'You should have kicked Martin out long ago, made him stand on his own two feet. I'll bet you take next to nothing off him. I'll bet you're still buying him the special things he likes to eat. You've even turned yourself into the little martyr, slaving in the burning sun while Martin is probably enjoying the surf.'

'I don't mind if he enjoys the surf,' she said steadily, 'it's the people he's mixing with I don't care about. People like *your* brother. How can you stand there and criticise Martin when no one could be more frivolous or ineffectual than Joel?'

'It's *you* I'm criticising,' Kyle said coolly. 'In any case, Joel is in entirely different position from Martin.'

'Of course,' she answered bitterly. 'There's no sense in our standing here trading insults. Kyle. I'll make a point of telling Martin you called.'

'So solemn, so frozen. I had no idea you were *more* than Scott Walker's secretary?'

She knew she flushed violently. 'Now it's my turn to tell *you* to mind your own business, Kyle!'

'I find it hard to put the sight of you two together out of my mind,' he drawled contemptuously, but the flame of a terrible anger seemed to leap out of his brilliant sapphire eyes.

'Scott Walker is a very kind man,' she insisted.

'Possibly,' there was the shadow of mockery on his lean, handsome face, 'but never in my wildest dreams could I see *him* as your lover. People think of you as a cool-blooded little creature, but you and I know differently.' He seemed to lean towards her and she arched back instinctively.

'At least I kept my passion for the one person,' Lynda said frenziedly, her upflung face shaded by the graceful winged branch of a tree.

He burst into bitter laughter. 'Yes, to put it aside after a peculiarly vivid two years. I was certain you loved me. You let me devour you night after night. Then, just like that, the fire burnt out.' He shook his jet black head mutely. 'I've asked myself what I'd do to you if we ever got this close again.' His tall, lean body seemed to quiver with suppressed violence.

'Scott said you looked like murder,' she told him, 'and you *do*!'

'How could Walker know?' He regarded her very attentively, instantly back to impeccable self-control. 'Don't tell me you're contemplating remarriage with a man old enough to be your father?'

Her smoky eyes darkened to slate. 'Am I supposed to stay in mourning for the rest of my life?'

'But how curious!' he flung at her. 'Mourning for the rest of your life. One mourns what one has loved, and all I gave *you*, Lynda, was excitement. I despise you, did you know that?'

'Heavens, no!' she almost whispered, staring into his blue eyes. 'I'm surprised you pay the slightest attention to me at all.'

'My mistake, my folly, my fallen angel.' He laughed, and it sounded terrible, deep in his throat.

'Go away, Kyle.' Everything about their intense lovemaking she remembered. It had been dazzling, another world that could not be possible with anyone else.

'Don't attempt to remarry,' he said, incredibly. 'I'll get it stopped.'

For a moment he looked so utterly ruthless she was floundering and out of her depth. In the past two years his dark and dominant male beauty had intensified as disturbing as some terrible dark force that was now being brought to work against her.

'You can't stop me from doing anything, Kyle,' she said at length.

'Darling, heaven knows, I can!'

He had always had the strongest possible physical

and mental hold on her, but now she felt afraid.

'I have no interest in Scott,' she murmured, more to protect him.

'Although you know he loves you. Sincerely.' This, in blatant mockery.

'Maybe the only man who truly has, except my father.'

His blue eyes flashed that peculiar fire. 'You said that like a little lost child. You're very beautiful, Lynda. You were only ravishingly pretty before.'

This encounter was leaving her spent and breathless, and she wished she was wearing her wide-brimmed straw hat so at least she could hide from his tense, lancing gaze. It had moved to her shoulders and her small breasts, her taut golden midriff, narrow, boyish hips and slender legs. It was like being stroked, but instead of comforting it was creating ripple after ripple of unbearable sensation.

'Will you *please* go away,' she repeated.

'I'm so sorry. Was I staring?.

'Tell me, then, what's wrong between you and Martin?'

'My dear girl, you couldn't help.' Kyle shrugged his wide shoulders, then looked up at the beautiful, cloudless sky. 'Have you an outing planned for tomorrow?'

'I can't think why you would want to know.'

He looked down at her abruptly. 'You seem to have forgotten the unhappiness you caused.'

'Maybe I have,' she said vaguely. 'I can't seem to feel anything any more.'

'Oh?' He put his hand on her bare shoulder and she drew in a deep breath.

'Always a game,' she said, and her flawless skin turned very pale.

'Anyone would think I had treated you very badly,' he said with hard irony.

'You did.'

He released her so violently she stumbled and almost fell, and he caught her again while she regained her balance. 'Sometimes I think you're clean off your head,' he muttered.

Lynda couldn't endure his touching her, his lean, beautifully shaped hand locked around her arm. 'No, I've kept my head, Kyle,' she said sharply. 'Some people take marriage seriously.'

'You *are* off your head,' he said, with a bitter, disillusioned expression.

'Haven't you married Olivia yet?' she asked quietly.

'Don't be absurd!' A cold disgust flashed from eyes that were half veiled.

'You *have* got your family where you want them.'

'My family accepted *you*.' He stared at her.

'Oh, no, Kyle, they didn't.' She still felt the frozen disapproval. 'Only your grandmother was kind to me.'

'You don't remember you were very unwilling to accept help?'

'You mean on the right way to dress and which people had the biggest wallets and all those trivial matters?'

'It's odd how you really hate people with money,' he observed tonelessly. 'I think we'd still be married if I were, say, a mildly successful accountant.'

'*No!*' She swung her head away and stared at the hectically flowering hibiscus hedge, grateful at least that no curious eyes could pierce their dense growth.

'So definite?'

'It wasn't just the power complex.'

'*God!*' His groan was that of a man driven. 'Allow

me to leave you with pleasure. Your kind of woman would break any man's heart.'

How could he say such impossible things! How could he look deep into her eyes with such anger? She wasn't insane. He had been unfaithful to her. He had dishonoured himself and her. The shock had been so extreme had she been in a poor state of health the onslaught and trauma might have killed her. Bad as the terrible blow of her parents' tragic accident had been, Kyle's infidelity had destroyed her utterly. When Christine told her she had been shattered. She and Kyle had often, perforce, made a joke of how Olivia almost literally threw herself at him at parties or whenever she invited herself to the family home. Sometimes she had felt desperately sorry for Olivia, even forgetting how deliberately unkind and patronising Olivia was to her, but eventually they had had it out, Olivia's story matching the one Christine had blurted out.

'Try to be mature about these things!' Olivia had taunted her. 'Kyle and I have been making love for years. If you didn't realise that, you're a fool. You can't imagine *you* would be enough for him!'

But of course she had, and the wound had been near mortal.

Kyle had already swung away and, half frenzied herself, Lynda ran towards the shelter of the house, dashing away the low branches of the jacaranda that like the poincianas had grown to a massive size.

'*Oh!*' Something thudded softly on to her shoulder and as she saw the thin green coils out of the corner of her eye she gave a strangled scream. She was going to freak out. She *knew* it.

'It's only a bloody tree snake!' Kyle threw it from her violently, all the muscles of his chiselled face tight and drawn.

'A . . . a . . . ah!' She was locked in continuous, convulsive shudders.

'*Lynda!*' He grasped her tightly by the shoulders.

In all her life she had never had a snake fall on her, and the revulsion was nearly making her hair stand on end.

'*Stop* that!' he ordered.

'I c-can't!' she stammered, knowing full well there were other snakes in that lush wilderness of garden. She had told Martin. *Told* him. She wanted to scream again but could not produce a sound.

'Come on, Lynda,' Kyle said sternly, and somehow that stirred her to tears. They clung to her eyes in a jewelled sparkle, then they fell on to her cheeks.

'It was harmless—I saw it.' He brushed the damp curls from her temples. 'I'm telling you, calm down. You'll collapse in a minute.'

Still the tears streamed down her face and with a muttered oath he lifted her and carried her off, helpless, into the house. She couldn't even fight him or cry out protestations.

'Where the hell do you keep the brandy or whatever?' he demanded in some kind of rage.

'The cabinet.' She was still breathing heavily and gulping, and he set her down on the sofa, looking back towards the cabinet, elaborately carved Eastern style. Concern lay on him, in the striking blue eyes and the bitter curve to his clearly defined mouth. 'Haven't you learned to relax your nerves?' he asked curtly.

Lynda sat upright at that, locking her small, slender hands together. How could he be so ruthless, so hateful, yet concerned about the small things? He shouldn't be here with her. She was realising that—too late. He had all the fascination and prowling menace of a leashed tiger.

He splashed a little brandy into a tumbler and came back to her. 'Here, drink it.'

'Thank you.' She took the glass from him, but her hands were trembling so badly the liquid shook.

'Listen,' he said quietly, and sat down beside her, putting his hand over hers on the glass, 'you can't let a common old tree snake shake you up so badly. Just get a grip on yourself. All right?'

She nodded her head slightly and he tipped the glass towards her mouth. 'I suppose you still haven't reconciled yourself to drinking alcohol?'

Its effect she could understand. The fine, distilled liquor ran down her throat, instantly depressing the rigours of faint hysteria. But now she was aware of the far greater danger, Kyle's lean, perfectly proportioned body beside her, his dark head tilted towards her own, the blazing physical attraction that had always been between them persevering like a lifetime penance.

'Good girl,' he said dryly, taking the tumbler from her and setting it down. An onlooker might have thought them lovers, for there was even a curious tenderness overriding his ill-concealed desire to make her suffer. 'How fragile you've become!' The blue eyes seemed to caress her like a violent kiss.

She could have said: 'I've suffered,' she she was too afraid to speak.

'Does Walker come here?' He drew her unresisting body across his knees.

'You can't do this to me, Kyle,' she whispered, like someone who had been hurt too much.

'Don't you think I feel contempt for myself?' He tilted her head back with his hand just as he had always done and as her eyes closed in acceptance of something unalterable, his mouth came down on hers.

It was like forbidden rapture .in exchange for her soul. Delirious, consuming pleasure that was truly alarming when one considered the *self* vanished. She had to have it on any terms, beyond resistance, beyond control, her body sinking back against his, losing itself in sexual passion.

Her breathing had slowed to almost inaudible. She was a girl rapt, locked once more in that strange, secret world which she had thought only she and Kyle inhabited; isolated but so complete, the very air enchanted.

One of his arms was locked across her body, below her breasts, its iron possession betraying the faintest element of cruelty, the body which he had known so completely without constraint, yet now he was hurting her. And surely he wanted to. Her little moaning breath fluttered into his mouth and he relaxed his hard hold on her without letting go. Rather he was mastering her with every passing second, the excitement running fathoms deep so that nothing had any meaning except this tumultuous coming together.

She wasn't even aware of the anguished passage of the years since he had last made love to her. Within moments he had effortlessly covered that empty, hungry distance, even wiping out the mortal hurt and humiliation that had devoured her brain.

'My God, but you move me—confuse me,' he muttered once.

Perhaps that was what it really was; a physical passion that literally destroyed. He turned her body sideways and unclipped her violet bra top, his hands immensely masterful yet caressing, covering the creamy slopes, his thumbs searching out the already erect nipples.

'Sweet,' he murmured, whether an endearment or an affirmation of the pleasure her body gave him, she did not know.

The stimulus was so erotic, so ravishing, she cried out, the soft, almost childlike cry abruptly cut off as he covered her mouth again. Urgency was flowing from both their bodies; the softness of hers, the hard maleness of his, a contrast that was perfect.

'If only we could go backwards in time!' He grasped a handful of her silky, wayward curls. 'Why didn't you love me?' His eyes were shamelessly desirous, but not loving. Some wounds were too deep for healing.

'Kyle——' her voice broke and immediately he scooped her up, carrying her through to the bedroom.

The process of bringing herself back to cold reality was beyond her. As a young girl she had never thought of herself as a sensual person. Indeed she had earned for herself something of a reputation for being very cool and exclusive when it came to the usual boy-girl intimacies. But Kyle had changed all that. He had unlocked in her an answering tumult of the senses, a certain wildness that astonished and engulfed her.

'Because you're *you*,' he had once told her. 'You make me what I am. I could never, have never, wanted a woman like I want you.'

Nothing made any sense at all, and she was too far gone to unravel his complexities. The body had a compulsive will of its own, at times too powerful to obey any directive from the brain. Kyle wanted her now, and he had won.

Their lovemaking was tormented and wildly passionate and Lynda knew that her body would ache for days, but she was too demanding of all his excesses to care. Incredibly, though he had said he despised her and she had wished fervently never to set eyes on him

again, their love-duel was ecstastic until they came to
the point when both of them were ready to scream for
mercy.

'*Lynda!*' He had to hold down her feverish,
writhing body.

'*Please!*' It was astonishing that she could speak at
all, but then neither of them could as their bodies were
taken over by orgasmic rapture, a power that was as
arbitrary as a great storm, lifting them to a peak, then
tossing them spent and exhausted back on to a dry
shore. A wasteland when reality returned.

Lynda lay with her hand over her eyes, the palest
pink sheet pulled up over her naked breasts.

'A bit late for that, isn't it?' Kyle came back to her,
dressed once more in the classic sand-coloured slacks
and easy cotton knit he had been wearing. He had
even had a shower, for his crisply waving dark head
was damp and his skin deeply tanned throughout the
year was like polished bronze.

'Back to business?' she said with no note of censure
or bitterness.

He sat down on the side of the bed and pulled back
the sheet, his mouth compressing when he saw the
marks on her body. 'I'm sorry. I didn't realise I was
being so rough on you.'

'Oh, yes, you did.'

'I suppose so.' He didn't attempt to excuse himself
again. 'Why, Lynda?'

'Why what?'

'I wish I knew your brain like I know your body. I
really do.'

'It's all my scruples,' she said. 'They weigh me
down.'

'Much good they did you this afternoon,' he pointed
out dryly.

'All you have to do is touch me. You know that.'

'It's just that you're not keen on marriage?'

'I don't like competition.'

'And what the hell is *that* supposed to mean?' She had put her hand over her eyes again and he lifted it away forcibly.

'Yesterday was yesterday, Kyle.' She couldn't meet his brilliant blue eyes.

'And what about today?'

'We all do mad things,' she shrugged.

'You bitch!' His tone changed to hardness and he stood up and moved away from her. 'I don't think I'll ever get over being married to a madwoman.'

'Mad as a hatter!' Lynda agreed, determined to keep the tears for later. 'Don't take it so hard, Kyle. A lot of people survive the death of their dreams.'

'Look,' he turned back to her violently, 'if I arrange it, would you see a friend of mine?'

'A psychiatrist?'

'You need help, Lynda.'

'Well, yes, but not yours, Kyle.'

'Even when I keep asking myself what the hell is *happening* to her?'

'You feel guilty?' She slipped out of the bed and stood naked before him briefly before she tied on her silk robe.

'I can't decide what I am,' he said at last. 'You're beautiful, intelligent, talented. Once you were even funny and the most wonderful company in the world.'

'Only I didn't have a chance.'

'You mean you didn't have any *guts*!' He caught the point of her shoulder and spun her towards him. 'Maybe I was deluding myself and you were never the things I thought you were.'

'Well, you know the saying, Kyle,' she told him.

'Love is blind. Only you didn't love me—you wanted me. There's a vast difference.'

He shook his glossy head. 'I'll have to leave all those fine distinctions to you. You could be even punishing yourself for so enjoying our sex life. You could have some crazy, puritanical streak for all I know.'

'Not today, anyway.' She gave a strange little laugh, conscious that the silk was dragging on her sore nipples. 'At least you won't make me pregnant.'

'Oh,' he glanced at her coldly. 'Are you on the pill?'

'That's *my* business.' Celibacy didn't require birth control pills.

'It had better not be Walker's,' he said in a dangerously soft tone. 'I'm giving you fair warning, Lynda. So you'll know where to place the blame.' He stood in the doorway and looked back at her, very tall and lean and strong, his blue eyes glittery and his chin with the ruthless Endfield cleft tilted arrogantly. 'You're wrong about my not taking our marriage seriously. You may have run like an hysteric. You may have put us through a divorce, but in my book you're still married to *me*, whether we ever live together again or not.'

'You're the one who's crazy, Kyle,' she said in a low, trembling voice.

'Well then, I guess I am. I have only two priorities in life. One is my work and the other is seeing you don't marry anyone else.'

While *you* retain your private life! She wanted to scream at him. She wanted to run and claw him—she of the gentle nature. But he had gone. A few minutes later from behind the curtain in the living room she saw his silver Daimler slide out of the drive.

She felt utterly unreal, her body still aflame with residual feeling, her heart beating frantically in foolish agitation.

Calm down. Calm down, she said to herself. How could Kyle possibly make more of a hell of her life than it already was? But then her pulsing body gave her the answer. He could take her when he wanted and he knew it. Unless she could depart this disastrous scene. As a wife she had fled before the terrible intolerability of sharing him. She would fare no better as a mistress. Maybe it *was* high time she let Martin fend for himself. Life had forced her into a situation where she had become her brother's keeper, but she could smooth his path no longer. It was a question of survival.

CHAPTER THREE

MARTIN arrived home very late Sunday night, but still Lynda was waiting for him.

'Good grief, not in bed?' He was very tanned, his thick golden hair bleached by the sun.

'I wanted to talk to you,' she said.

'Oh, sweetie, not now!' Martin walked past her and set his bag down in the hallway. 'I've had a terrific weekend, but I'm tired now.'

'Then in that case you'd better listen.' She stared at him, recognising him for what he was, a spoilt only son. Their mother had adored him, and he *had* been an adorable child. Lynda she had loved, of course, but just as Lynda had been her father's favourite, Martin had been their mother's son. Lynda stared at him with enormous grey eyes.

'Well?' Martin was obviously rattled by her long regard.

'Kyle Endfield called here yesterday.'

'Really?' Martin didn't look so much surprised as dealt a body blow. 'To see you?'

'It was you he wanted to see.' Lynda looked down and tied the cord of her robe again, plainly appalled by the expression on her brother's face. 'I got the distinct impression he was concerned about a few things.'

'Such as?' Martin spoke aggressively, which was his way when he was worried.

'I don't know, Martin,' she said unhappily. 'He didn't confide in me.'

'God!' Martin lifted his hand and struck himself a light blow on the temple. 'What a lunatic relationship you two have always had! Listen, I could lose my job.'

'How, Martin?'

'*How, Martin?*' He mimicked her low, shattered tone. 'Ah, the hell with it, I suppose you've got to know. I've been doing a little bit of borrowing.'

'*What?*' Lynda's small oval face whitened and she looked shocked out of her mind.

'You heard!' Martin shouted at her with hostility. 'God damn it, where do you think I've been getting the extra money from? Not much, just a hundred dollars here and there. It's easy when you know how.'

'Easy with the Endfields?' Lynda's legs threatened to give under her and she moved back into the living room, sinking blindly into a chair. 'You attempted to treat a man like Kyle as a fool?'

'Oh, calm down, will you?' Martin stabbed an agitated hand through his thick blond hair. 'I've always put it back. Anyway, I've only taken it when things have been crucial.'

'You mean when you've lost at the races?'

'I've won a lot too,' he said with terrible jauntiness. 'Kyle still cares enough about you not to hurt me.'

'I can't believe this,' Lynda muttered.

'It's true. The only reason I'm telling you is because I have no choice. If Kyle is on to me, and I can't see that he would ever concern himself with trivia, I'll need you to bail me out.'

'I won't be doing it, Martin,' she said.

'Oh yes, you will, kiddo.' He tried to laugh, though his lightish blue eyes looked terrible. 'Anyway, how do you know something was wrong? It could have been quite a different matter. He might have been using it as an excuse to see you. Joel reckons you're still in his blood.'

'Don't speak to me about Joel,' she said icily.

'Joel is a very agreeable feller!' Martin stood up, then walked to the drinks cabinet. 'I say, who's been drinking the brandy? Had good old Scott here, have you?'

'Scott has never visited me at home.'

'You're very proper, aren't you, pet?' Martin tried woefully to give her his winning smile. 'It's extraordinary how you're such an old stick-in-the-mud and I seem to get caught up in all sorts of adventures.'

'Daddy always said you had no common sense,' she said bitterly.

'He was never very keen on me,' Martin agreed.

'He loved you, Martin.'

'You were the one who really mattered. He left you the house.'

'He left you the money—all gone. You've been incredibly foolish, Martin.'

'It wasn't all my fault,' Martin said. 'You seem determined to be ordinary, but I want to *be* somebody. I want to hit the big time.'

'By stealing?'

Martin flushed violently and he clenched his fists in baleful anger. 'If you were my brother instead of my sister I'd sock you for that one!'

'A brother might give you back, Martin, what you deserve,' she retorted coldly.

Martin shrugged his thin shoulders and the flush died out of his face, leaving it deathly green. 'I haven't done anything too wrong, Lyn, I swear it. Just a little borrowing here and there. I never thought for a moment Kyle would delve into things at *my* level. I mean, I scarcely see him. None of us do. We're just the hirelings.'

'What a fool!' Lynda rolled her head back, unsurprised it was aching. 'I'll guarantee Kyle knows the companies' assets right down to the last cent. I was once in the Rolls with Sir Neville and he had the chauffeur turn it inside out hunting up some spilt change.'

'Eccentric. Everyone knows he's eccentric,' Martin muttered. 'That's his reputation—an eccentric billionaire.'

'And how do you think he got that way?' Lynda demanded, her quiet tone suddenly going up the scale. 'Encouraging the staff to help themselves?'

'There's no need to shout!' Martin swallowed his whisky neat and in one belt. 'The most Kyle can do is fire me, and I don't think he'll even do that. Not when he hears my story.'

'What story?'

'I've been helping you out. That's it!' Martin suddenly looked healthier, grabbing at his nerve. 'You desperately needed money for something or other. Stop sitting there looking so upset and let's try to figure something out. You needed money for something. *What?*' He looked at her piercingly.

'Forget it, Martin,' she said grimly. 'You damned well won't hide behind me another day.'

'Don't hand me that, Sissy,' Martin said brutally. 'In your own way you're just as big a pushover as Mum. Maybe all women are like that—the maternal streak. Hey, stop looking at me as if I'm Dracula! I'm Martin, your brother, remember? And what have I ever done that's so bad?'

Lynda stood up abruptly, a small unconsciously gallant figure. 'How much money have you taken, Martin?'

Martin told her quite innocently.

'Oh *God!*' She bowed her face into her cupped hands.

'Peanuts!' Martin cried coarsely. 'You're acting as if I've embezzled a fortune.'

'You mean you can't see theft for what it *is*?' Lynda whispered, looking more distressed than ever.

'We don't even know what Kyle came for,' Martin persisted. 'Let's not talk about it until we do.'

'I know it was that.' Lynda looked at her brother with her eyes full of fears. 'What's going to happen to you, Martin?'

'Nothing,' he said cynically. 'Not with you around. Joel told me a strange thing at the weekend. He said the family thought Kyle only needed time to forget you, but they were all wrong—he, Christine, his mother. You're there in Kyle's bloodstream, whether he wants it or not.'

'He despises me,' Lynda told him, with a strange calm.

'Has he actually said that?' Martin demanded, feeling easy in his mind that Kyle never had.

'Just yesterday.'

That shook Martin badly. 'You never did know how to handle him. You let yourself be manipulated, Joel said.'

'Joel is a snake,' Lynda said tersely.

'You're the only person I know who thinks so. He's handsome, maybe not in Kyle's class, he's witty, good company, and he's absolutely rolling in beautiful money.'

'Then go to him as a friend,' Lynda suggested.

'I'd die first.'

'Because he's not a friend, Martin. Friends are for when you're in real trouble. You could go to Perry tonight. He might read you a lecture, but he'd help you. Joel would laugh in your face.'

'*Please*, Lyn,' Martin turned a pleading face to her. 'You've never failed me before.'

'I can't help you now, Martin,' she said.

'Then I hope you're going to take the time off to sit with me in court.'

Her small, high-cheekboned face looked grief-stricken. 'Why didn't you think of that when you took the first hundred? *How* did you take it? I'd rather starve than take a penny off the Endfields.'

'But then you're a bloody fool.'

'That's your opinion, Martin. Where are your ethics?'

'You can't enjoy ethics, Lynda,' he sneered. 'They won't take you out to dinner, or yachting, or get you in with the right people.'

There was silence while Lynda sat there despairing, and finally she said, 'I hate to say this, Martin, but I don't think I've known you at all. What's more, you deserve to be punished. It might bring you to your senses.'

'It might make me drive off a cliff!' Martin shouted. 'I can see you're upset, Lynda, but whatever you say, I know you're going to help me. You'll blame yourself for the rest of your life if you don't.'

At the office Scott felt the weight of Lynda's troubles but found that, much as he wanted her to, she wouldn't confide in him. The days went past in a constant state of tension, and Lynda found it very difficult to concentrate on her work. Martin, too, was tormented by the waiting. Kyle had taken a direct flight to Tokyo to rejoin his grandfather and he wasn't expected back for another ten days. So in Martin's words, they 'sweated it out endlessly'.

'We could be mistaken, you know that?' Over and over he tried to reassure himself. 'Are you *certain* he acted as though something was wrong?'

Lynda didn't have the heart to tell him Kyle had told her she should have evicted him long ago. Yet Kyle wasn't blameless. He had known all along that despite Martin's 'cleverness' he wasn't a strong character. Then too, there was Joel's bad influence. So long conditioned to making excuses for Martin, Lynda knew in her heart there wasn't one. Martin's aims and ambitions were all wrong and she had achieved absolutely nothing by trying to be kind and understanding. Her sheltering and bolstering of Martin had only been continuing a familiar pattern. The only disagreements she could ever remember her parents having were over her mother's 'mollycoddling' of Martin.

'You'll ruin the boy, Julie!' How often had she heard it. 'You can't be forever solving the boy's problems.'

She had picked up where her mother left off, which was why she was now riddled with guilt.

'*Lynda?*' Scott had to address her twice before she heard him. 'Let me take you home.' It was after six and they had been working overtime.

She wanted to say she would rather take a taxi, but caring was written all over Scott's long, rather distinguished face. 'That will be nice!' She smiled at him, which was a mistake, because her smile was one of her greatest assets, though she totally failed to grasp it. Once it had flashed out constantly, now it was rare.

Scott almost sighed aloud with relief. For a moment he had been certain she would reject his offer. This last week she had seemed more unreachable than ever and twice as desirable. Just being able to see her every day had transformed his life.

They drove for quite a while before Scott spoke. 'You can't go on like this, Lynda. Don't you realise it?'

'I'm so sorry, Scott,' she apologised. 'I was miles away.'

'Torturing yourself, from the look of you. Please, can't you tell me what's wrong? Don't feel I won't understand—I would.'

She realised she had to say something, but the truth was just too terrible. 'I'm worried about Martin,' she finally managed. 'I'm worrying that he's living far beyond his means.'

'Can't you speak to him?' asked Scott.

'He won't listen to me.'

'Then why don't you lock him out of the house? It is *your* house and it might be better that way. It's about time Martin worked things out for himself.'

'He can't manage now, Scott. If I tried to turn him out I don't know where he would go.'

'But surely he's earning a good salary? I know for a fact that Endco employees are well paid.'

'The trouble is Martin wants to live the good life,' she sighed. 'He keeps telling me how fantastic life is at the top, but he's very, very wrong about that. The Endfields had more difficulties than anyone else I've known. In one way it's a paradise, in another a prison.'

'The point is,' Scott maintained firmly, 'if Martin is going to continue to run around with Joel Endfield he's going to make a mess of his life. How two brothers could be so extreme! Endfield at thirty-three or four has the role of magnate sewn up, whereas his brother is held by everyone to be just a playboy.'

'I used to feel sorry for Joel,' admitted Lynda. 'For a time.'

'What really happened to your marriage, Lynda?' Scott slowed down as they approached a red light. 'Just two short years, and you were very young.'

'I've decided I'll never get married again.'

'Don't say that!' Scott put out his hand and gripped her arm as though he could stave off such a tragic decision. 'One mistake may have set you back, but you have your whole life in front of you. I assume you want children?'

'Unfortunately I do.'

'I want to marry you,' Scott said. 'I know I'm a good deal older than you, but at least I can promise you I'll do everything in my power to make you happy.'

It was hard to find the right words. 'I'm very fond of you, Scott,' Lynda said gently, 'but you deserve a woman's whole heart.'

Uncharacteristically, instead of sitting behind a big car, Scott passed it. 'Let's just focus on what we've got. You say you're fond of me and I love you. You don't want to marry anyone else?'

'I may not be allowed to,' she said tightly.

'And what's that supposed to mean?' Scott evidently decided he couldn't talk and drive well at the same time, so he pulled off the road. 'Come on, Lynda. You've said something strange, now answer it. Sometimes you're so darned mysterious!'

'Maybe there are so many things I don't particularly want to talk about. It's . . .'

'What?'

'Kyle has told me he'll take good care I don't marry again.'

Scott's stifled oath was audible. 'How the devil can he do that?' His quiet face was filled with anger and an unmistakable degree of confusion.

'I'm frightened of Kyle,' Lynda confessed,

'For heaven's sake!' Scott's voice sounded odd. 'Does he know anything about us?'

'What is there to know?' she lifted her large, smoky eyes.

'That's right.' Scott fell speechless. 'They're ruthless devils, you know,' he said eventually, and even shuddered. 'Has he actually threatened you?'

'He has.'

Scott looked appalled. 'So if he can't have you, nobody else can.'

'He doesn't want me,' Lynda pointed out with a funny little laugh. Now it was obvious Scott was frightened of Kyle too.

'Then why the tyranny?'

'It's natural in a tyrant.'

'Good Lord!' Scott looked as though his nerve had all but failed him. 'Looking back to that function I might have realised that deep down he's a very primitive man. You belong to him and that's that.'

'So you see, Scott,' she said gently, 'you'd be showing good sense if you put me firmly out of your mind.'

Scott glanced swiftly in his rear vision as though expecting some sinister private investigator to be parked several feet from them. Nevertheless he said gamely, 'My dear, I'll help you—I swear it.'

When he set her down outside the house he looked at her with deep emotion, then leaning forward kissed her mouth. A very nice kiss, Lynda thought as she walked inside. A parting kiss, maybe, as he sent her off to the Tower.

The sound of voices made her recoil. Martin's and Joel Endfield's unmistakably. It was a very attractive voice, yet it had the effect of paralysing her. It really was time to give up. She had made it clear to Martin that he was not to invite Joel to the house.

'Ah, here she is!' Joel strolled through to the hallway, his right hand cradling a drink. 'Lynda dearest, how *are* you?'

'Joel.' She looked at him coldly, but he totally ignored her, bending his head and kissing her on the mouth.

She drew away in disgust, but he only smiled. 'You're beautiful, did you know it?'

'I hope you're not staying, Joel.'

'Of course not,' he said soothingly. 'Martin and I are going out. He's just getting changed.'

'I see.' She went to move past him, but he caught her by the shoulder. 'Why rush off? I haven't seen you for years.'

'Personally I've always hoped it would be never again.'

'Oh, I say!' The malicious hazel eyes sparkled. 'You never used to be nasty.'

'I guess a little rubbed off from your family,' she shrugged.

'You never did understand us, did you?'

'I tried for a while.'

'Yes, a sweet little thing you were too. Trying to make friends with Christine when she was as jealous as hell of you.'

'Christine was?' Her grey eyes were sceptical. Joel always had been an extravagant liar.

'Yes, and you were too naïve to know. Chris and I have never hit it off, but even you must have seen how she adored Kyle. He always had time for her, listening to her little problems and giving her advice, but you came along and took him off her.'

'How ridiculous!' she protested.

'You really are *hopeless*, aren't you? Surely now you're older and presumably a little wiser you can see how things were? From out of nowhere Kyle produces this beautiful little girl that nobody knows. The shock of it was immense, not only to Mother but the rest of us as well. I mean, he had never even mentioned you, then in the next breath he was going to marry you—a schoolgirl, and a very mixed-up little girl at that. Nice as you were, you made it perfectly clear from the beginning that you were going to lead your own life. And that, my dear, was your mistake. The family washed their hands of you for good.'

'You mean they couldn't forgive me for not being Olivia.'

'I mean they couldn't forgive you because you were taking Kyle off them. More and more each day. He had a great passion for you I'm not even sure is cured.'

'Well, I went, Joel. Which was what you all wanted.'

'You don't even sound bitter.' He looked down at her curiously.

'Defeated. What should have been a dream turned into a nightmare.'

'Well, isn't that what a mad passion is?' he moved restlessly. 'Even I could see what Kyle saw in you.'

'Yes, Joel,' Lynda stared through him and back into the past. 'You tried hard enough to make trouble.'

'But Kyle always trusted you. The fact that I was attracted to you meant nothing to him.'

'Because it meant nothing to me.'

'So that's why I hated you.'

'You're not normal, Joel,' she told him quietly.

'Because I always hanker after the couple of things I can't get?' The hazel eyes were insolent, touching on her face and body. 'You know, you're even better looking? Obviously a broken marriage didn't affect your looks. All the little gauche bits have worn off. You've even learned how to dress.'

'I always had good taste, Joel,' she corrected him. 'I just found it a bit horrific at times paying out a fortune for clothes.'

'Yes, I know!' He rolled his eyes theatrically. 'Mother never could understand it. She wanted a daughter-in-law who would attend all the showings with her and get a reputation for being the second best dressed woman in town. You, my dear, were a real failure, and you couldn't even keep your political views to yourself—so earnest, so desirous of improving the workers' lot. Why didn't you just settle for being a sophisticated and amusing little butterfly? You had everything going for you—young, a beauty, even a lady. You had Kyle crazy about you when he could have had any woman he wanted, but no. You wanted to be a little do-gooder with a mind of your own.'

'The exception in your house,' Lynda said drily.

'You should never have lived at home,' Joel told her.

'Well, of course that goes without saying, but Sir Neville wouldn't hear of anything else.'

'You didn't imagine you were going to take Kyle from his own grandfather?' Joel looked at her with a triumphant smile. 'What my grandfather wants, my grandfather gets. Besides, Kyle is the only one of us who matters to Grandfather. Uncle Graham and Uncle Nick, all the cousins, Chris and I are utterly useless to Grandfather. We're not brilliant at anything. We can't stand up to him. Even you could do that. Grandfather mightn't have liked you, but at least he respected you.'

Lynda stood looking at the handsome, weak face. The Endfield features were good, but much, much diluted from Kyle's strength. Still, now and again Lynda had always had a sneaking sympathy for Joel.

'Why don't you at least *try* to find something you're good at?' she asked him.

'Pardon me, pretty one, I like being idle.'

'No, you don't, Joel.'

'There you go again!' he mocked her. 'When are you ever going to learn that you can't win people around to your way of thinking?'

'You do see you're unhappy?' She just let her smoky eyes rest on him.

'So who isn't? I mean, *you* are. Let me see. Chris is nearly suicidal. Kyle is pushing himself so hard and fast I don't think he's ever going to live as long as Grandfather. The only one I know who seems utterly self-satisfied is Mother.'

'Yes.' Mrs Endfield did indeed seem to fill in her days happily.

'And you do understand why we couldn't have you?'

'It doesn't matter now, Joel.' Lynda went to turn away. 'But your family was never the main issue. You all tried to make me live your way of life, but you would never have beaten me.'

'So who *did*?' Joel looked genuinely astonished.

Lynda shrugged. 'There was only one person who could ever do that, and that was Kyle.'

Joel took another big gulp of his Scotch. 'But, my dear little girl, you've been the only thing in life Kyle couldn't handle. He would have married you if Grandfather had cut him off without a cent. He was nuts about you, and you seemed the same. In fact the two of you together used to irritate Chris and me something awful. You know, locked up in your own private world.'

'Well, it's over,' Lynda said flatly.

'Who was the character who drove you home?' Joel went to the door and looked out. 'Walker?'

'Obviously, you saw him.'

'In love with you like everyone else?'

'No, Joel.'

'It looked like it. I must tell Kyle. I think he'll take a dim view of Walker's having the nerve to kiss his ex-wife.'

'Oh, hi there!' Martin, beautifully groomed and glowing, strode through to the entrance hall. 'Like another drink, Joel, before we go?'

'I suppose I might, seeing you're driving.'

'You'll excuse me?' Lynda tried to speak pleasantly.

'Just a minute, Lyn.' Martin caught his sister's arm, then turned back to Joel. 'Go in and help yourself. I won't be a moment.'

''Bye, darling.' Joel waggled his fingers at her. 'If you ever want someone to take care of you, think of me.'

Lynda didn't even bother to answer. The time in her early married life when she had had to repulse Joel's little intimacies! She had always suspected the motive for his seeming attraction. Anything that belonged to Kyle, Joel seemed to crave. Maybe such family situations always turned out a mess. Kyle was so naturally gifted. He had been a Rhodes scholar, a fine athlete, and the apple of his grandfather's eye. To a man like Sir Neville to whom high achievements seemed to be important Joel in his own way had suffered all the time. Whatever he did, and some things he did well, Kyle did them much better.

No wonder I so often felt sorry for him, Lynda thought.

'Well, at least you and Joel didn't come to blows.' Martin remarked happily. 'I'm sure, given a little time, we can work this whole thing out.'

'If you want to think that, Martin,' Lynda said wearily.

He drew her into the small sitting room and closed the door. 'Listen, I think we've got the whole thing wrong. I've been sort of pumping for a little information and I've come to the conclusion that there was little more to Kyle's coming here than the desire to see you.'

'I told you what he said, Martin.' Even Lynda felt a lift of the heart.

'Joel says he's perfectly happy with my work.'

'But maybe he's just checked it.'

Martin grasped her tightly and kissed her on the cheek. 'I think we've been worrying for nothing. Kyle isn't on to me at all.'

'Please, God, that's the case,' Lynda said fervently. 'Have you put all the money back?'

'I had to take out a loan.' Martin was almost back to being jaunty. 'Look, love, I made a mistake, a big one, but I've had such a fright I promise you I'll never do such a foolish thing again.'

'I'd be happier, Martin, if you said *dishonourable*,' Lynda told him. 'Stealing has more consequences than being found out. It's a breakdown of your character.'

'I promise you, Sissy, I'll never do it again.' He kissed her again. 'Now, I must be off. Joel and I have been invited to a party.'

'A bit early for a party, isn't it?'

'We have to pick up the girls first. I tell you, my girl is really something!'

'Well, just you damned well see you don't get her into trouble,' she cautioned.

'Would I? *Would I?*' Martin only grinned at her chilly comment. 'All the girls are on the pill these days. Didn't you know?'

Yes, I know what women have to do, Lynda thought, when men won't even face the consequences of their actions. Had she a vicious nature, she would have revenged herself on Olivia somehow, but she could never turn into something she was not.

Kyle was 'nuts about you', Joel had said. Well, it had been like that for two years then Kyle had become bored with her. Maybe it was impossible for a man to resist an opportunity, especially a man of such sexual power. Olivia had made it perfectly plain she wouldn't rest until she drew Kyle back to her bed, but however much he condescended to be her lover it was quite apparent he didn't care to marry her. What arrogance!

A few days later Martin rang Lynda at the office.

'Can you come over?' he burst out in a rush.

'Over where?'

'To Endfield Towers.'

'Of course I can't, Martin,' she said fiercely. 'What's the matter?'

'Kyle wants to talk to you.'

'About what?' She was locked once more into extreme agitation.

'He's on to me, Sissy,' Martin said desperately.

'Oh, my God!' She knew then there would be a price to pay, and she would have to pay it.

CHAPTER FOUR

KYLE's secretary ushered her into the inner sanctum, avid little glances glimmering through the proper secretarial demeanour. As she had been fifteen years with Endco she was quite aware of Lynda's identity, though she appeared decidedly at a loss as to what to call her. Finally she abandoned trying to call Lynda anything, but smiled reservedly and held back the door of the huge executive office.

'Ah, Lynda.' Kyle rose from behind a very impressive desk and came around to her. 'I suppose it was a great personal sacrifice for Walker to let you go?'

'I said I had a headache,' she told him.

'How prophetic!' His deeply blue eyes were glittering with mockery. 'Joel tells me he's decidedly attached to you.'

'*Joel* is?' she challenged him shortly.

'Joel greatly admires you, we know. I'm talking about Walker. I would have thought a man like that would have known how to abide by the rules.'

'You mean that bit about not taking an interest in me?'

'Thou shalt not covet thy neighbour's wife.'

'May I sit down, Kyle?' she asked.

'I'm terribly sorry.' He drew forward a chair. 'Of course you can.'

'You might tell me very quickly what I'm here for.'

'Let me remember first.' He went back to his chair behind the desk, facing her. This was his background, big business, extreme affluence, and he looked greatly impressive without making the slightest effort at all.

'It seems Martin has been manipulating certain funds,' he told her bluntly.

'He told me.' She bowed her head in shame.

'Look at me, Lynda, so we can get to the bottom of this.'

'All right.' With a certain hauteur she lifted her cloudy dark head. 'Martin has been very, very stupid.'

'Criminal,' he agreed.

'Then why did you take him on?'

'Maybe to keep an eye on you.'

'Oh, Kyle, *do* be serious,' she said abruptly.

'You interest me, Lynda,' he said. 'You're highly intelligent, yet you're shocked by the facts. I hired Martin basically to keep a finger on you.'

'Why?' A pulse began to hammer at the base of her throat.

'You're my wife, Lynda.'

'We're divorced.'

'*You're* divorced.' His blue eyes were brilliant with hostility. 'I never wanted it, but even I can't change the law. You put yourself in the solicitor's hands and I had to go along with it.'

'Because our marriage was a mockery.'

'Thank you for telling me what it was. Has it never occurred to you I was only biding my time to get you back?'

'You're playing a game with me, of course,' she said flatly.

'You little fool!' His vibrant voice flicked at her like a whip. 'I don't like being made a fool of, Lynda. I don't like being backed into an untenable position. You fled me like a little hysteric—God alone knows why. I realise it wasn't easy for you trying to cope with my family, but I thought you were woman enough to do it. Certainly you always stood up to my grandfather. You even managed to hold your own with my mother, which isn't easy. I shall never begin to understand why you behaved in such an incomprehensible manner.'

'Well, it's over now,' she flashed at him. 'You're a dictator, Kyle, just like your dear grandfather. I always knew it in my heart.'

'Thank you, Lynda,' he drawled suavely, 'I think I'll almost enjoy proving it.'

'What are you going to do about Martin?' she said fiercely. 'Where *is* he?'

He gestured towards the outer offices. 'I haven't got him locked up. Yet.'

'You see, it was *my* fault,' Lynda explained.

'Go on, do tell me,' he drawled.

'I was having difficulties,' The sudden flush on her high cheekbones betrayed her agitation. 'Martin did it for me.'

'So he said.' The voice was very cold and cutting.

'He's put it back, hasn't he?' she asked nervously, moistening her softly sensuous mouth.

'Oh, yes.' His eyes seemed to be following the tip of her tongue.

'He'll never, never do it again, Kyle.'

He smiled briefly—a very unpleasant smile. 'We can be sure of that. What a swine he is, really.'

'Oh, *please*!' Glittery tears sprang into her eyes.

'You know.'

'You're not being fair to him, Kyle.'

'To blame you,' he said bleakly. 'You who refused a small fortune.'

'Times have changed, Kyle. I needed money right now.'

'Oh, shut up!' he said curtly. 'You're almost blindingly honest, and your brother is flawed.'

'Aren't you going to take a little of the blame?' she asked futilely.

'Anyone with even a grain of sense wouldn't attempt to rob me. But then we're not even talking about sense. We're talking about principles, ethics.'

'Have the Endfields always behaved so well?' she asked bitterly. 'I know it's disgraceful what Martin has done, but your grandfather has sent a lot of people to the wall.'

'One has to expect that in business. The big people are eating up the little people all the time. It's a fact of life. However, I would like to point out to you that he has never attempted to rob his friends.'

'*What* friends?' she cried heatedly. 'He may have had a dazzlingly successful business life, but you must realise a lot of people hate him.'

'You mean they're terrified of him,' Kyle said smoothly. 'People sometimes feel like that when they're confronted by inexhaustible energy and shrewdness. My grandfather is what he is, but I'm afraid we must return to Martin's guilt.'

'So hang him,' Lynda said emotionally, and her mouth started to tremble.

'Not allowed.' Kyle shook his shapely head. 'I've thought about this for a long time, and the only way Martin is going to be able to avoid the sheer misery of jail is for you to offer retribution yourself.'

'But I've got nothing!' she stammered. 'Not a lot. I could sell the house.'

'Darling,' he said acidly, 'I don't want you to do that—how ridiculously easy! No, *Miss* Reardon, I've thought of the perfect punishment for the crime. I want you to come back to me. You may not be exactly sane, but you're a very interesting girl. Then too, you have a pretty formidable sex appeal. I'm much too busy to go out at nights chasing other women, so I'd like my own wife back.'

She didn't answer him at all. She couldn't, her eyes were abnormally large and shimmering like crystal.

'I've shocked you.' He sounded deeply ironic.

'We could never make it together, Kyle.' She shook her head wonderingly from side to side. 'I can't come back to you, ever. I can't—I can't!'

'But, Lynda, it's your destiny. Your unhappy fate.'

'No.' She shook her head again. 'I can do no more for Martin.'

'All right, then,' he said coolly, as though it didn't really matter, 'I'll bring an action against him.'

'You couldn't,' she said brokenly. 'Not if you ever loved me.'

'Forgive me, darling, the question is if you ever loved *me*.'

She lifted her head and his brilliant glance struck at her; anger, arrogance and contempt.

'There's a devil in you, Kyle,' she whispered.

'Especially when I have you in my arms.'

A soft shudder went through her, the remembered arrowheads of flame. 'Have I time to think about this?'

'Why, certainly.' His brief smile was exquisite, a flash of white that illuminated the brooding severity. 'I'll get my secretary to make us a cup of coffee and you can tell me then.'

Martin was frantic to find out what had been decided, but Lynda refused to speak to him on the phone. Let him sweat it out, she thought bitterly. Let him be punished as Kyle has set his heart on punishing me. By the time he arrived home shortly after six, Lynda really did have a headache.

'Okay, I understand you couldn't speak on the phone. But what happened?' he demanded of her, jerking muscles betraying his deep agitation.

'How about repainting the hallway?' she said ironically. 'Just who the hell do you think you are, Martin? You leave everything in the house to me, all the bills, all the maintenance, all the providing, and now you expect me to underwrite your shady activities!'

'You mean you *won't*?' Martin sat down quickly as if the strength had gone from his knees.

'Can you tell me why I should?'

'I get it,' he said harshly. 'You're going to forget you're my sister.'

'I should have forgotten it a long time ago. Instead I picked up where Mummy left off. You've been allowed to believe you can do anything you want and when there's trouble, someone else will bail you out.'

'I tell you, Lyn,' he said fiercely, 'I'll never be so stupid again. Sometimes I think you're the only person in the whole world who really is my friend.'

'Perry is your friend,' she said shortly, 'although even Perry has had to give up calling. But no, you had to take up with the one person who could ruin you. *Has* ruined you.'

'So he's going to prosecute?' Martin dropped his head in abject misery.

'I'm going to remarry him,' Lynda said.

'Sweetheart!' Martin's face lit up magically.

'I don't want to, Martin,' she said, and her lovely, sensitive face hardened. 'You can't know what it was like before.'

'But it was the family you hated. Not Kyle.'

'I've never hated anyone, Martin,' she said tiredly.

'Mine isn't that kind of a nature, and anyway, I wouldn't want it to be. I'm more interested in the bonds of loyalty . . .' Her voice broke and she started to cry.

'Then don't marry him,' Martin fell on his knees in front of her. 'I know I'm a rotter.'

'Not a rotter, Martin. Weak.' Angrily, she dashed the tears away.

'Then at least give me a chance to do something about it.'

'Such as?' She put out a hand and brushed it over his shining blond hair.

'Is Kyle forcing you to marry him?' he asked.

'Yes.' Lynda swallowed on the lump in her throat. 'If I marry him he'll make other arrangements for you. You'll be sent to a sudsidiary company in Central Queensland where you'll be expected to work very hard and I'm sure you realise you'll be kept a close watch on.'

'You mean he'd *tell* them?' Martin demanded, turning deathly pale.

'Of course not. Kyle has told no one. He's just going to make sure you shape up in the way he wants.'

'I will!' Martin apparently saw with great clarity what would happen to him if he didn't. 'I swear I'll turn over a new leaf.'

'That's fine,' Lynda said painfully. 'I'd hate to think what might happen to you if you didn't.'

'So you're going to marry him?' Martin remained kneeling, but he was making another of his lightning transitions.

'It looks like it, doesn't it?'

'Don't you worry,' Martin said happily, 'it will all work out!' And the most extraordinary part was, he seemed to believe it.

Once the wheel of fortune was set in motion things happened quickly. Lynda handed in her resignation to Scott and he reacted with shocked incredulity.

'I can't believe this,' he said faintly. 'Why, you told me yourself you were frightened of the man.'

'It's very hard to communicate what I feel,' she said evasively.

'Then why allow *me* to get my hopes up?' Scott jumped up from his swivel chair and went to the plate glass window, looking out.

'I'm sorry, Scott,' she said sadly. ''I didn't think I did. I always try to be honest.'

'Then tell me the truth now!' Scott was uncharacteristically worked up. 'How about your hare-brained brother? Has he something to do with this?'

'Of course not!'

'It looks a bit like that to me.' Scott's pale cheeks were flushed. 'You said you were worried about him.' Lynda didn't think she could go on sitting in the chair.

'I'm remarrying Kyle because I love him.'

Scott took that very badly indeed. 'But you were never happy with him.'

'I was—ecstatically.'

'I don't understand you, Lynda,' Scott said grimly. 'I suppose I never did.'

'Believe me, I never had any intention of hurting you,' Lynda said quietly.

'Well, my dear, you *have*.'

So it was all over, her short working life. And now her confrontations with the Endfields were about to begin. A few days later while she was working fitfully in the garden, a magnificent chauffeur-driven Rolls-Royce Silver Spur purred solemnly into the driveway. The uniformed chauffeur sat behind the wheel, and a divinely groomed, handsome mature woman reclined against the impressive back seat.

Kyle's mother.

For an instant Lynda had the absurd impulse to head for the river, but there seemed no way out. The chauffeur brought the magnolia Rolls to a complete stop, then hastened out of the car to hold open the rear door as though on no account could his passenger be expected to open the door herself. Lynda almost applauded the style. How nice it was to know that one could still get a decent motor car for around two hundred thousand dollars.

'Lynda!' Mrs Endfield called.

'Anthea.' Lynda felt like shrieking aloud. Here was the woman who had given her hell, the sort of mother-in-law sons-in-law would gladly murder but their daughters-in-law were supposed to accept and keep their mouths shut.

'My dear!' Tall and very, very slender, Anthea incredibly offered a matt cheek, and though she seemed to be hysterical inside, Lynda just barely touched her lips to the exquisitely kept skin.

'Could you not have warned me?' Instantly it was *on*. Anthea delighted in catching people when they were not at their best; under hair-dryers, or feeling ghastly or even, as Lynda was doing, emptying the garden rubbish.

'My dear, I didn't exactly know I was coming here,' Anthea lied blandly. 'May we go into the house?' The expression that accompanied the request implied that Lynda might have the bad grace to keep them standing out in the garden.

'Of course. Have a cup of coffee with me.' Fortunately Lynda had always had a sense of humour, even where Anthea was concerned.

'A nice place you have here. It should fetch a high price on today's market. Some of these old houses were very stylish, and I don't think one can beat verandahs for coolness.'

Inside it was indeed lovely and cool and Lynda was glad she had taken time to fill the house with fresh flowers. Anthea looked at the arrangements attentively and allowed herself to smile. She too loved houses and gardens, though obviously one needed household staff for anything that looked like work.

'You've changed, you know, Lynda!' Anthea put her handbag down and gave Lynda a good stare. 'Fined down. You were always very slender, but now it's easy to see that elegant bone structure.'

'You look well, too, Anthea,' Lynda returned somewhat dryly. 'Please go into the living room and sit down. I'll excuse myself for a few moments and wash. Summer makes everything grow so hectically it's rather difficult keeping up.'

'You should get a man in, dear.' Anthea's expression registered Lynda's peculiarities.

It was too much to expect that Anthea would realise gardeners cost money. Anthea had come from a very wealthy family herself and she had only upped her lifestyle with her early marriage. But even Anthea had been crushed by life. Her husband, Richard, Kyle's father, had been killed in a terrible accident at a mine site. There had always been the rumour that it had been sabotage, but after a lot of formal and informal interrogation and many convictions aired, the tragedy, involving one of the great cranes and causing the death of two men, had been blamed on the maintenance department. A grave charge, though it had everything pointing to it, that was denied heatedly for many long years by the Chief Engineer. But whatever had really happened. Richard Endfield had been killed instantly, as had the brave young man who had raced to save him.

With these thoughts going through her head, Lynda's whole attitude softened. Anthea had suffered. She had heard the story of Anthea's breakdown and the grief that had broken her. Christine, her youngest, had been little more than a baby and Kyle had been twelve—a particularly difficult age to lose a father, but Sir Neville had quickly established himself in dual roles; father and grandfather, idol and head of the family.

Very quickly Lynda made a few repairs to her appearance, changed her shorts for a skirt, then considerably freshened up, she went back into the living room where Anthea was upending a piece of porcelain and reading the marks.

'Royal Worcester.'

'One of my mother's favourite pieces.' Lynda looked tenderly at the beautiful porcelain figure.

'Do sit down, my dear,' Anthea suggested, the hostess wherever she went. 'I must confess I was absolutely stunned when Kyle told me you and he were getting together again.'

'And how do you feel now?' Lynda sat down in an armchair and fixed the older woman with clear grey eyes.

'It still sounds incredible.' Anthea rearranged a fold in her skirt. She was wearing the most beautiful silk dress in the loveliest shade of wine-red. In her early fifties, she was carrying her age in the most graceful way possible, making no attempt to look 'younger' but achieving an easy drop of ten years. Lynda had never seen her look less than perfectly groomed, even when the whole household had been disturbed in the middle of the night by an intruder. Belted into a sumptuous robe, her thick black hair swanning around her instead of standing on end, Anthea had looked the unending envy of her friends. Now she was regarding Lynda with still dazzling blue eyes. Kyle's eyes, though the rest of his looks were pure Endfield.

'I didn't even know you two were seeing each other again,' Anthea murmured, clearly having a great deal of trouble accepting it. 'But of course, he never got over you.'

Lynda laughed shortly. 'Nor I him.'

'Yes, it certainly seems that way.' Anthea appeared to make a firm effort to get hold of herself. 'I came here today, Lynda, to tell you I very much regret our differences in the past. I see now I misread my own son's deepest feelings. I adore Kyle, as you know, and I suppose like most mothers I was jealous when he turned so completely to you. Even my poor Christine was frantic with a sense of loss. Kyle has been so many things to all of us. He's the strong one in our family. He has always known where he's going, what he's doing. We might have accepted that he was right about you instead of our senseless running battle. The thing is, my dear, we all felt robbed, and instead of sharing in Kyle's joy we collectively decided to blame you for taking him from us.'

'But I never did that!' Belatedly Lynda began to realise the origins of the family resentment.

'Of course you didn't.' Anthea's tone was clipped and short. 'Not consciously, but you do remember Kyle was deliriously in love with you. There were times when his allegiance to you strained the rest of us to the limit. I mean, *I* am Kyle's mother. I brought him into the world. He is my pride and joy. He has every quality of my dear husband's, every quality his brother and sister lack, though I love them dearly—I have to. Kyle is Kyle. I can say no more. Even Grandfather was surprisingly jealous.'

'Sir Neville?' echoed Lynda.

'Really, dear, don't be obtuse! We all thought we had the perfect girl lined up.'

'Olivia,' Lynda said flatly.

'Of course.' Anthea raised guileless blue eyes. 'Olivia's mother was my bridesmaid. I bounced Olivia on my knee.'

'You did?' It seemed utterly preposterous that Anthea had bounced anyone—but then, Lynda thought wryly, there's a lot I don't know.

'She's my godchild. Then too, she's a very clever girl, and she was so much one of us. She would have understood about Kyle.'

'But then, it seems, he didn't love her,' Lynda pointed out. 'Or at least he didn't want her as a wife.'

'No doubt about that,' Anthea heaved a heavy sigh. 'We were quite wrong about Olivia, and there have been times lately when I've had to look at her in astonishment. Of course, hanging around waiting for Kyle to ask her to marry him has been a strain.'

'I'm surprised to hear that,' Lynda offered dryly. 'I thought she was quite capable of tricking him to the altar.'

'No one could make Kyle do anything he didn't want to do.' Anthea gazed down at her gloriously beringed hands. 'I'm very much afraid Olivia has been wasting her time, but unfortunately for her she made her choice in the cradle.

'Undoubtedly it was unfortunate for me as well.' Much as she tried, Lynda's sensitive face could not remain tranquil. 'Olivia did everything in her power to break up my marriage.'

'*Please*, dear.' Anthea stroked her white forehead helplessly. 'We must forgive and forget.'

'I don't think I'll ever quite forget,' Lynda said quietly.

'Actually you're being rather sweet,' Anthea allowed. 'You always were a kind girl, and as fond as I am of Olivia, I realise she treated you badly. But then you always had the upper hand. Olivia had her sharp tongue and the family for allies, but *you* had Kyle. Why in the world do you think we all behaved so badly in the first place? I'm saying it now and I shall never say it again. I detest having to explain myself in any case. Families *can* be a plague to the young marrieds. At least I was blessed with a wonderful mother-in-law. We made mistakes, I know, but I'm welcoming you back into the family gladly. I was wrong to interfere in my son's life. You are fulfilment to him—not me, and certainly not Olivia, poor girl. Now she will just have to go off and find someone else. That's the way of it when couples remarry.'

'Thank you, Anthea,' Lynda said gently, regarding the older woman's becomingly flushed cheeks. 'It will be wonderful to have your blessing.'

'Yes, yes,' Anthea replied, and jumped up. 'Kyle said you're coming to dinner tomorrow night. Grandfather will be free then. We must make our plans. Of course we can't have a big wedding like the first time, but a small one can be enchanting as well. What about a very soft, misty lilac? I was at the most wonderful showing the other day. The bridal dress was antique lace, but the bridesmaids wore this incredible gauzy lilac with little silver camisoles of antique lace. It would suit you perfectly. Really, you may have been terribly lonely, but there's no doubt a little unhappiness has improved your looks. You're a genuine beauty. I was one myself.'

'You still are,' Lynda said lightly. And a genuine humdinger as well. Kyle had promised her as part of their contract that they would find a house of their own. It was either that or being eaten live again.

The Endfield mansion was set in four acres of some of the highest priced real estate in the State capital. It was a modern palace, especially designed for the sub-tropics by one of the most gifted architects in the world whose own house was in Singapore and Lynda had always thought it the most beautiful and compelling house possible. It was a very large house on anyone's scale and the architect had understood perfectly the demands of the climate and the sort of house required for anyone who like Sir Neville entertained on an incredible scale.

As usual, at night, the grounds were well lit, and Harry, on the gate, saluted smartly as Kyle drove through.

'Just the family?' Lynda asked to break the electric silence.

'Never *just* the family,' Kyle said dryly. 'A couple of Grandfather's old cronies, Frank Arnold and Matthew Dixon. You know them.'

'I feel profoundly strange,' Lynda confessed.

'Never mind. You look exquisite.'

She had indeed taken her appearance very seriously. It was almost a case if you can't lick 'em, join 'em, or at least bow to compromise. Instead of attending to her own highly manageable hair, she had made an appointment at an excellent salon, and the result was the difference between looking delightful and looking great. Even her dress had been an unaccustomed extravagance, a satin-striped chiffon in a dusky shade of mauve, almost a jacaranda. It lent a mysterious blue haze to her smoky grey eyes and not surprisingly her appearance gave her the additional confidence she needed. The very first time Kyle had taken her home she had been shaking with stage fright. Now she was a woman, a pretty darned disillusioned one and no longer terrified of not creating a good impression. Kyle wasn't remarrying her for love. He had saved up this vengeance, so she was free to stand apart and treat the family as she treated everyone else, with courtesy but not greatly caring whether they approved of her or not. That had been yesterday, and she considered it a mercy she was all grown up.

'Lynda!' Sir Neville greeted her with two hands on her shoulders and a kiss on the cheek. She might have been a favourite young female relative and not the girl he had disapproved of so heartily—probably did still.

He took her hand and drew her across the entrance hall into a living room of very grand proportions. Very little had changed. The beautiful parquet floor was defined in the seating areas by magnificent Caucasian rugs, the rich dark background the perfect foil for the jewelled masterpieces, the creamy-toned walls and woodwork, the pristine whiteness of the large modern sofas and armchairs with a judicious sprinkling of antique appointments. It was a highly sophisticated yet imaginative room, and Anthea had been responsible for its luxurious comfort. Wonderful as the room was, it was obviously meant to be lived in, as were all the rooms of the house, and Lynda supposed had Anthea not been a rich woman she could have made a career for herself as an interior decorator of rare talent.

Anthea was there, her eyes the brilliant blue of her dress, Joel trying to look the picture of the smooth operator but only succeeding in looking supercilious, a very pretty blonde girl Lynda didn't know, Tracy Forrester, Joel's latest 'friend', Kyle's Uncle Nick with his wife, Erica, the hard line of her mouth matching the assessing look in her eyes, Sir Neville's two colleagues, who greeted Lynda with unmistakable pleasure and old-world gallantry, and finally Christine with Blair Neale, her long-time admirer.

Blair gripped her hand sincerely and smiled back, but Christine made absolutely no attempt at friendliness, rather projecting a long-ago hostility she couldn't yet get under control.

'Now, Lynda my dear, come over here and tell me what you're going to drink.' One would almost have thought Sir Neville was enjoying himself, but Lynda knew the old man better.

They had drinks in the living room, the little tensions dissolving in general conversation, then they went in to dinner.

They're telling me they're actually going to make the effort to get along with me, Lynda thought. Placating Kyle was what it was all about. Two years ago they had thought they had written her off, but here she was again, Kyle's intended bride for the second time. Obviously she had power, and power was what they all admired.

Dinner was superb; an entreé that featured the delicious crabmeat of the famous Queensland 'muddies', followed by a chicken sauté with white wine and mushrooms and various vegetable accompaniments, an orange and rum-flavoured mango mousse decorated with whipped cream and toasted slivered almonds, and for those who had any space left, the cheese board, very much Sir Neville's favourite. Coffee was served, as usual, in the library along with any liqueur one fancied, but after exactly twenty more minutes of mixed conversation Sir Neville made it perfectly clear the women could take themselves off elsewhere. In Sir Neville's world, men were the true aristocrats and women on a par with subnormal children.

Lynda decided, as usual, that he was the most ruthless and brutal old devil imaginable, albeit a very formidable and handsome one, but Anthea rose happily, having given up every effort to be seen as a man's equal.

'I rather thought we might discuss the wedding,' she exclaimed.

'*Must* we?'

'What did you say, Christine?' Anthea looked back at her daughter, somewhat embarrassed.

'I couldn't care less!' Christine muttered. With a beautiful mother and two exceptionally good-looking brothers, Christine was that unhappy thing, rather dull, though her mother did everything in her power to help the young woman achieve an approximation of good looks.

To Lynda's way of thinking, a pleasant expression and manner would have worked wonders.

'We haven't decided anything yet,' Lynda returned.

'You must have been keeping your meetings very much secret?' Erica Endfield sat down opposite Lynda and subjected her to another of those assessing stares.

'Maybe it was wise,' Lynda pointed out gently, remembering how this woman had used to bait her.

'Tell me,' Erica smiled tightly, 'do you think it will work out better this time?'

'Of course it will!' Anthea came to Lynda's rescue unexpectedly. 'We're all older and wiser now and I think it's quite apparent Kyle very much needs her.'

'Oh, spare us!' Christine sighed.

'If you're going to be disagreeable, dear,' Anthea said mildly, 'you can run along.'

'Where, Mother?' Christine's hazel eyes were bright. 'I'm not such a hypocrite I can pretend I'm glad Lynda is coming back.'

'Coming back where, Christine?' Lynda asked evenly.

'Why, here!' Christine raised her straight eyebrows. 'Hell, you know what Grandfather is like!'

'Unfortunately I do.' Lynda settled back quite comfortably. 'However, he may have to do without us. I've told Kyle we must have a place of our own. I'm quite sure we can put a phone in every room.'

'You may try, my dear,' Erica Endfield eyed Lynda speculatively, 'but I think you'll find Grandfather will have his way. He truly needs Kyle every other minute.'

'And he may have him—during the working day.'

'Not exactly a conformist, is she?' Christine asked ironically. 'Say, don't you remember what happened the first time you were married?'

'There are some people who just don't know when to give in.'

'But truly, dear,' Anthea leaned forward and gripped Lynda's wrist, 'Grandfather will expect you to live here. You have a whole suite of rooms to yourself.'

'But since I'm marrying Kyle and not the family I'd rather be on our own,' Lynda persisted quietly.

'Are you nuts or something?' Christine asked. 'Can't you grasp the realities of life? Grandfather is all-powerful. He may not be too fond of me or poor old Joel, but he idolises Kyle—I thought you grasped that long ago.'

'I know you're all rather neurotic about Kyle,' Lynda agreed.

'I'm not ashamed of it.' Christine looked back at her with positive hatred. 'I relied on my brother very much. He was my hero and my greatest friend, and then *you* came along.'

'Surely you expected Kyle to marry some day?' Lynda asked.

'Yes, and you know who!'

Lynda met the venom with calm eyes. 'Well, she certainly had her opportunities, but nothing apparently came of it.'

'You're very generous, Lynda,' Anthea said. 'Now I think of it, *I* wanted my own home, but Richard, like Kyle, was indispensable to his father. At the time I think I was particularly upset. I've always had a great talent for houses and I wanted to do something very special for just the two of us. But alas, that was never to be. By the same token, my dear,' she added in a harder voice, 'don't expect it to be easy. Grandfather detests relinquishing his hold on anything.'

'No wonder he despises you,' Christine told Lynda hoarsely. 'You've never treated him with the respect he's used to.'

'Can one despise a person who knows their own mind?' Lynda asked.

It appeared to confound Christine momentarily and she fell into a pent silence, while Anthea cleared her throat.

'Incidentally, I see you're wearing your old ring?'

'Yes.' Lynda pressed the great sapphire on her left hand, reliving for a brief moment the time Kyle had told her he would 'ram it down her throat' if she every tried to return it to him. He had been very, very angry and she, trembling, had thrust the beautiful ring back into her handbag and out of sight. Until tonight.

'I've been talking to Nick,' Erica said. 'He only wants what's best for Kyle. Of course we don't always see things in the same way.'

It looked as if from a fairly good start it was going to turn into a horrible evening.

'Won't you play for us, Anthea?' Lynda asked. Anthea was a very accomplished pianist, but even if she had been dreadful Lynda would still have asked.

Anthea stood up almost gratefully and nodded. 'I was only thinking the other night, you were one of the few people who ever asked me, and really, you know, I could have been very good. Aunt Charlotte was a concert pianist.'

Sweet little blonde Tracy had been listening to all these exchanges with all the head motions of a spectator at a tennis match. Finally she looked at Lynda with dazed eyes and not a little admiration. Surely there couldn't be steel running the length of that slender, feminine body? In the meantime she had better rethink her plans for marrying into the Endfield family. Not for love nor money would she dream of setting up house with this lot.

Fifteen minutes later Nick Endfield and old Matthew Dixon came back into the living room, lured by the wonderful sound of the music. It had taken Anthea over so that she forgot Sir Neville, her dead husband, the pending remarriage of her beloved son— everything.

'I say, isn't she splendid!' Quietly Nick Endfield took a place beside Lynda. 'Poor old Anthea! She's had the best and the worst of it. By the way, you look extremely attractive tonight, Lynda. I always did say Kyle was a lucky man.'

Anthea played on, and Christine, always insensitive to her mother's musical talent, stumbled away to find Blair. She had a good mind to marry him and ruin his life!

CHAPTER FIVE

LESS than a month later, Lynda became Mrs Kyle Endfield for the second time.

'Not terribly good, were you, the first time?' Joel turned her face up and kissed it, the driving force in his life envy of his brother and everything his brother possessed. Like a wife.

By some miracle Lynda had had her way over the wedding. It was small and quite private, and she had rejected the idea of a much bigger reception.

'Can't you see how you're disappointing everybody?' Kyle asked her suavely.

'They had their spectacle four years ago,' she told him.

Anthea, determined on mending bridges, played the loving mother and the lean-on-me-for-support mother-in-law, and even Christine had been persuaded not to say or do anything that could be considered extreme. All in all it went off rather well, apart from Sir Neville's saying he would have their suite of rooms redecorated.

'A new start!' He nodded towards Lynda emphatically, daring her to destroy the fragile harmony. She didn't. She merely lifted her eyes and what Sir Neville saw in them made his own eyes sparkle. Mutiny was always very boring, but fairly easy to put down.

A second honeymoon couldn't be expected to last as long as a first one and as far as Lynda was concerned the shorter the better. This wasn't any real marriage.

This was mockery. The only person who had gained anything was Martin, and he was going to be cut off from civilisation for at least two years. However, it was scarcely likely Joel or his crowd would make an attempt to get to him.

'Don't worry about me, Lyn!' Martin had told her at the wedding, his expressive voice fervent as a zealot's. 'I'll make you proud of me yet!'

'At least do better than you've done so far!' Kyle had cut him off rather harshly, while all the delighted conversation droned on around them. Apparently everyone was finding it hard to believe Lynda and Kyle were very much in love again and actually remarried. Only Kyle accepted it without question, his manner low key but exuding possession. Lynda had been very young before, but it was high time she settled down for good.

In the week Kyle had 'free', virtually big brother and not in the least lover-like, he reasoned that as they didn't have the time to sail Sir Neville's dream yacht they would hire a yacht up North and cruise the glorious Great Barrier Reef islands, he the skipper and Lynda the crew.

Lynda had allowed him to rattle off the cruising ground, the guaranteed sheltered achorages, the white sands fringed with casuarinas and pandanus, but where once Lynda would have thought this the perfect choice, the two of them so very closely together surrounded by so much breathtaking natural beauty, she had absolutely no intention of stepping on any yacht with Kyle. He had taken enough control of her life and she wasn't going foolishly into any no-win situation. The days of marital rights were over when a woman had to accept any demands her husband made on her. Kyle had agreed to accept her terms for the marriage contract; any sleeping together had to be by mutual agreement, so she was determined to stave off any humiliatingly early disaster by insisting on staying on Caprice, a jewel-like tropical island wholly owned by the Endco subsidiary, Capricornia Estates, and run as a luxury tourist resort. That way, instead of dangerous 'togetherness' there would be a good deal of activity, nightly entertainment and lots of other holidaymakers to dilute the straight company.

When they finally arrived by helicopter after a wonderfully panoramic trip from the mainland, the manager was there to meet them. He tucked Lynda carefully into the little train that ran from the helicopter pad, past the beautiful beach-front cabins, especially designed to blend into the luxuriant natural environment, and on to the luxury apartments, that sitting back against the palm-studded hillside had a magnificent view of the incredibly blue lagoon, the ocean beyond and an exquisite little coral atoll called Luana that one could almost walk to at low tide.

Of course there had to be a drawback. They had been allotted *the* honeymoon suite, and though the bed appeared to be unparalleled in size it wasn't fitted with some sort of dividing board in case the newlyweds turned out to be incompatible.

Kyle himself seemed phenomenally untouched by the spirit of romance. 'I think I'll bag the bed tonight,' he told her. 'You must realise that I'm six feet two and you're very much smaller. There should be plenty of room for you on that day-bed.'

'Suppose we take it in turns?' Lynda didn't even bother to reproach him.

'Splendid.' He lounged casually on one elbow, arrestingly elegant even in resort clothes. 'Is this to be classified as a trial remarriage?'

If he could be hardboiled about it, she couldn't. 'This isn't some joke between us, Kyle,' she said poignantly, her smoky eyes huge. 'You forced me into this trendy, open marriage when I'm well aware you don't love me and probably never did. I suppose it's the business man in you. You want to keep the record straight. Once Mrs Kyle Endfield, always Mrs Kyle Endfield.'

'And dismiss any ideas about another divorce for ever!'

'What a curious man you are!' She gave him a flashing look of scorn. 'I'll keep *my* part of the bargain.'

'Bless you, darling.' His blue gaze touched silkily on her face and her lightly clad body. 'Then you can expect me see me taking lots of long, exhausting swims in the lagoon.'

'You won't have any problem adjusting.' Lynda kept her face cool, but little tingles of apprehension were running up and down her spine. Just how far could she trust him to keep to his word? How far could any woman trust any man, for that matter! The war was ancient and bitter.

For almost a week they indulged in every sport the island offered—sailing, scuba, snorkelling, tennis, mini-golf, extensive walking, exploring the coral gardens, even birdwatching.

'I'm having a wonderful time!' Kyle told her, so superbly fit and handsome a lot of the women thought it worth the money just to watch him.

Lynda, for her part, found herself for most of the time exhausted. She realised she was just falling into bed while Kyle read quietly, but her physical strength wasn't comparable with his.

'*Up!*' he ordered suddenly.

'What time is it?' she whispered, stunned.

'We're seeing the Outer Reef this morning. I've been talking to Jeff and the conditions are just right.' Powerful arms carried her to the shower while she lay as helpless and bemused as a child rudely awakened. He was bearing this cracking pace far better than she was, and last night they had stayed up so late at a little private party a much travelled French couple had given in their apartment.

'Oh, *please*, Kyle,' she begged him, fearing he was about to do the unforgivable thing and turn the cold shower on her.

'Shall I help you off with your nightdress?'

'*No!*' she exclaimed frantically, and pushed with quivering strength against his powerful arms.

'Surely you're not being modest, darling? I can see right through it!'

'You shouldn't be looking,' she said severely.

Really, this was dreadful, and she was trying at all costs to keep her barely veiled body from sinking in delicious compliance against his. The torment was exquisite and he was holding her helpless.

'Let's talk about our wedding contract,' he said pleasantly, the hard musculature of his body impressing itself on her soft, woman's flesh.

'Get out of here, Kyle,' she said moaningly, unable to make the slightest impression on those cleverly locked arms. She should have had the sense to take a crash course in judo or at the least self-defence.

'But I'm only helping you, darling. Be still, now, like a good girl.' He pushed one of the lace straps of her nightgown off her shoulder, then the other, so soon her breasts were free, barely touching his chest.

'You can't do this to me. You just can't!' Her voice

was ragged with an instant hot rush of desire.

'Really? I thought it was rather sexy.'

'It's not sexy at all. It's an invasion of privacy.'

'Not yet, but I suppose we're well on the way!'

The nightgown slid to the marbled floor and she saw the mockery leave his face as the tension built up inside of him. 'Tell me you want me,' he ordered.

His eyes were so blue and intense unconsciously her body thrust against his. 'I *don't*, Kyle,' she denied herself wildly. 'You always think you can have just what you want and just when you want it.'

'And *you* don't?' He had her so tightly she thought her bones might break.

Tears formed in her eyes and her trembling mouth opened. 'Please, Kyle!'

'Oh, my God!' He threw back his head and closed his eyes. 'Sometimes I think you're not quite human, like some cruel little goddess.'

His expression was so agonised she stared up at him in bewilderment, thinking of their lost love, the passion and the moving tenderness, the way they had responded so quickly to one another's every mood. For long moments she almost forgot Olivia, not even understanding why Kyle had turned away from her. She had been certain he loved her. Certain that he wanted nothing more than the dizzying rapture they shared together. But, in fact, she hadn't known him at all. While sometimes her love for him had threatened to overwhelm her, he had felt the need for another woman.

Olivia.

When Kyle finally looked down at her, he didn't see hunger in her enormous, smoky eyes, but glistening pain.

'What is it? Can't you tell me?' One hand reached up to a cup the side of her face, a tender, protective gesture, almost entreating.

Lynda stood perfectly still, frightened to make the slightest movement, her breasts crushed against the dark bronze flesh of his rib cage, every dangerous part of their bodies locked. She had only to offer him the slightest sign. But she wouldn't.

'All right, Lynda,' he said, almost wearily, and turned aside to pick up the shower cap. He dragged it over her tumbled curls and before she had time to gasp spun the cold tap so that both of them were inundated by cascades of cold water.

'*Beast!*' she shouted at him above the rush of water, but he ignored her, stripping off his single garment and now turning on the hot water.

'I haven't got any room.' She was obliged to fall back against the tiled wall, but it was obvious he didn't care. The water crashed over his splendid male body and then he was gone, leaving her in clouds of steam, inside and out.

On the trip to the Outer Reef Lynda expected him to be on edge with her, but he was perfectly relaxed and as always, in company, the most contented husband in the world. Fortunately the trip was so blazingly beautiful it overcame even Lynda's deep and perplexed feelings, and she began to respond, almost exultantly, to this wonderful blue world, the incredible blue of the sea, the brilliant blue of the sky. Blue—such a lovely, healing colour.

'Bit of all right, isn't it?' Jeff, their skipper, announced in glowing tones.

'Marvellous!' Lynda didn't even notice Kyle's arm come around her shoulders.

On this highly fortuitous early morning when conditions were just right a great section of the outer reef was exposed like a giant raised platform in the glorious blue sea. It ran for perhaps six miles, almost two hundred feet wide, some sections worn smooth from the constant action of the big surf and other sections a wondrous mingling of coral colours. The Outer Reef, the main part of the greatest coral reef in the world, extended in a great arc, enclosing nearly seven hundred islands, continental islands, such as Caprice, Magnetic, Royal Hayman and Lindeman, and the true coral atolls and cays.

'There you are, Mrs Endfield. Thirty million years old!' Jeff had to shout to get above the roar of the mighty Pacific. It crashed against the great coral rampart with a frustrated roar, throwing up a dense white cloud of elemental power.

It was as spellbinding as it was awesome, the tremendous waves racing at the reef as if they meant to pound it to powder, then crashing against its mighty bulwark with a thunderous roar of defeat. Out of the brilliant blue deep the waves rose in solid emerald peaks, higher and higher, the white spray shot through with every colour of the rainbow. If another wave was higher, surely it would engulf them!

Instinctively Lynda retreated against Kyle's shoulder and he wrapped both arms around her and hugged her to him much as if she were a mesmerised child. It was certainly thrilling, but all along was the fear. The glittering green waves rose like mountains, flaunting their power, pillars of fury that almost shut out the golden sun. Lynda admitted the phenomenal spectacle, but she could not quite control the mortal fear. She kept thinking of the tide changing or a wind blowing up. She imagined this awesome scene during a cyclone and thought there could be nothing more gripping or terrible. The ocean was meant to strike both love and fear in men's hearts.

Looking down at her, Kyle could see she was both fascinated, undistracted from the mighty spectacle, and acutely nervous. Her cloudy dark hair, like his, was damp from the heavy spray, whirling tightly into curls, and the flawless skin, gold from the sun, was downed with salt. She seemed quite unaware he was holding her confidingly close, her slender body warm and alive.

Conversation was impossible and they explored the crystal clear pools in silent concentration until Jeff yelled to them that it was time to leave. There were only ten well defined openings in the reef, and though he had made this trip many times before over the past twenty years Jeff had a sailor's healthy respect for the world's trickiest navigation.

'I'll always remember this,' Lynda murmured, ravished all over again by a truly unique sight. Seabirds swirled all around them, gulls and terns and petrels, and she felt dwarfed by this limitless blue world, the brilliant sun that warmed their faces and bodies. Jeff was as tanned as old leather and there were masses of lines around his bright blue, ever watchful sailor's eyes.

Safely inside the reef again the sea was serenely smooth and so crystal clear they could see rainbow-coloured fish skimming some little distance below the water. Other jade-coloured islands shimmered in the distance, enclosed by their rings of exquisitely white sands.

'This just has to be one of the most beautiful places in the world!' Lynda threw out her arms to the sparkling sapphire blue waters.

'You'll go a long way to beat it!' Jeff smiled at her expressive face and the depth of feeling in her voice. She was flushed and the salt breeze had whipped her dark hair into a purple-sheened aureole around her lovely young face. He had known Kyle Endfield since he had been two years old, but this was the first time Jeff had met his beautiful young wife. Everyone had heard of the divorce, of course, everyone who knew the family, that was, but looking at them both Jeff was certain their marriage would work out. He had never seen a man keep a more protective eye on his wife than Kyle, nor a woman who melted so gracefully. It made him feel good.

Kyle was an accomplished windsurfer, indeed he was the best windsurfer on the island, but still Lynda continued to take her lessons with the hotel's coach. It was exhilarating skimming across the waves and she had experienced surprisingly fewer unplanned duckings than most of the other novices. Kyle could sweep past with a nonchalant wave on an advanced design of sailboard, but Lynda was determined to become as good as any woman could be. Her light weight suited her particular board and she had the advantage of being a natural at water sports.

Eventually, of course, it had to happen. She was being far too adventurous for an amateur and as her confidence grew disproportionately to her sailing ability she found she was eager to leave the beach farther and farther behind.

That afternoon the off-shore wind gave the sea a deceptively mirror-calm appearance and although the coach had pointed out potentially dangerous situations Lynda fell into the trap of thinking she could handle her rig in such ideal conditions. There were other sailboarders out, but whereas they were content to sail in circles Lynda had the sharp urge to spurt ahead.

From out of nowhere the gentle puffs of breeze became gusts almost catapulting her into the water, but although she moved quickly into the correct recovery procedure she realised immediately that she was being swept out to sea. The rig had so tripled in power there wasn't even the chance she could sail parallel to the shore.

Where were the other sailboards? Where were the boats? It just wasn't possible no one had noticed her. Besides, there were plenty of sunbathers basking on the beach. Kyle had been speaking to the manager up at the main building nearby. If he came down on to the beach as he had promised he couldn't fail to notice she was being borne swiftly seaward.

Fool! She, who had always prided herself on her common sense. Just because she had taken to the sport like the proverbial duck to water it didn't mean she had the experience to handle stronger winds. She knew the distress signal. She even knew the procedure for a self-rescue operation, but the rig was moving so swiftly she couldn't even think of collapsing it. The only thing she could think of was abandoning the rig. She was a good swimmer, but she didn't have all that much stamina. The farther from shore she sailed, the more difficult it would be to swim in to the point where she could be rescued.

It was the only time she truly welcomed Kyle's wealth. She had to abandon, and do it at once. Kyle could easily replace a sailboard, but he might have some difficulty getting his wife back. Though why, in fact, he wanted her utterly confused her.

In such glorious summer weather she was wearing only a one-piece swimming costume, but the constant spray and her alarm appeared to cause a considerable drop in her body heat. She was cold.

Swim for it. You can do it. Yet she was in an ecstasy of fear she would suffer a cramp. Water was her friend. She had always loved it, but the sea was wild. How strange that she could drown when she loved the water too well. The waves were half blinding her, glistening one after the other, and she began getting sharp mental images of Kyle.

The cramp struck first as a single spasm, then as a rapidly constant agony.

'Well, that's it!' she told herself fatalistically. A pity in lots of ways.

'I love you, Kyle,' she muttered aloud on the slightest breath. It was doubtful anyone would see her bobbing head or the arms she tried to lift; gentle ripples had become choppy waves. She might have foreseen this would happen, but Kyle was always so superior to her in every way she had wanted to show him she could do it. Phil Hunt, the coach, had given her the extra confidence in herself, and how he would bitterly regret it. Poor Phil!

The thought of what Kyle might do to him kept her afloat. *Why* hadn't Kyle loved her? The heat of anger warmed her body. Up until the very minute Christine had told her, her eyes regarding Lynda with every kind of hostility, triumph and pity, she had thought she and Kyle shared a love that grew stronger every day. She had thought even the air blessed them.

'I wish she'd never told me,' Lynda thought. But then Olivia had chosen to tell her too.

While she was sinking rather dreamily into despair, a speedboat was ploughing steadily through the waves.

'There—over there!' Kyle pointed imperiously, his voice harsh with strain.

'Yes, sir.'

Philip Hunt could not help realising he was in terrible trouble. He altered direction, then glanced swiftly at his passenger, but Kyle Endfield had already gone over the side, striking out strongly towards his wife in the water.

'Thank you, God. *Thank you!*' said Phil in rapturous relief. Endfield was making Olympic time, but the greatest thing of all was that Lynda had waved her arm.

When he reached her she was gasping and coughing but her small, bloodless face registered no panic.

'I have you.' He wondered if he had said it aloud.

Phil brought the boat up beside them, not daring to speak. These were the Endfields. They owned the island and there had been almost a fatality.

Endfield's strong arms lifted his young wife almost clear of the water and Phil hauled her in.

'Are you all right, Mrs Endfield?' he asked, almost desperately. Lynda at lessons, but now she was Mrs Endfield.

Rather gallantly she tried to nod at him, but her whole body was shaking and gasping for air.

'Where's the blanket?' Endfield asked him curtly.

'Here, sir.' Phil felt as though the strength was leaving his own body.

Lynda felt the warmth of the blanket folded around her, then Kyle lifted her into his lap. 'Get us back to the beach,' he told the anxious young man without turning his head, and Phil sprang into action. The last thirty minutes had been without question the most wretched time of his life.

News travels fast anywhere and on an island with the speed of lightning. The beach and the jetty were crowded with guests and staff, all of them desperate in their urgency for good news. In the midst of such beauty and the holiday atmosphere everyone had been totally unprepared for disaster, and when it became apparent nothing dreadful had happened, the air rang with spontaneous, heartfelt cheers.

Lynda herself over the worst of her shuddering, but far from normalcy, managed a few feeble waves, but at the graven look on her husband's dark face, the crowd soon broke up. It was clear that Endfield, as much as his young wife, had sustained severe shock.

The doctor came out on to the balcony to speak to Kyle.

'I've given her a sedative. She'll sleep. Now, what about you?'

Kyle merely shrugged. 'I'm fine.'

'You don't look it.'

'I just need a little time.' A muscle was jumping along the taut jawline. 'Thanks, Frank.'

The doctor nodded and picked up his bag. 'I'll look in again in the morning.'

They walked together to the door and the doctor looked again into that handsome, tightly controlled face. 'Take my advice, Kyle, and have a drink or two. You need something to help you recover from such a stressful situation. Lynda is *all right*.'

'Yes, she is,' Kyle breathed deeply, managed his first smile and let the doctor out.

At three o'clock in the morning, Kyle Endfield still stood looking out at the dark tropical garden. Moonlight gilded the great fronds of the palms and there were shadows all along the magnificent hibiscus hedges. He had found it impossible to sleep.

'Kyle?'

The sound of his own name made him turn swiftly. He heard quite clearly the gasp of fright, and then she screamed.

'Lynda. *Lynda!*'

When she came to Kyle was shaking her and she

knew she must have been having a nightmare. His body was bent over her and he had her by the shoulders.

'Everything is all right—I'm here.'

'Oh!' She tipped back her head and stared directly up at him. Only a single lamp glowed, but it bathed his dark features. Curious, his vivid blue eyes were dark pools, almost black. 'I've been dreaming,' she said.

'And hey, little one, you were *screaming*!'

'It was the cramp!' she all but wailed. 'I was reliving the pain and the panic.'

'Actually you kept your head remarkably well. Are you quite sure you weren't trying to drown yourself?'

'None too poetically.' She missed the betraying tightness around his mouth and the peculiar emphasis in his voice. 'What time is it?'

'Three o'clock, if you're really interested.'

'And it seems to me you haven't been to bed.' She lay back abruptly, still feeling drowsy and spent.

'I thought I'd keep an eye on you,' he told her.

'You saved my life, Kyle,' she said quietly.

'You didn't consider ending it?'

'Don't be absurd!' Even in her bemused state she was shocked at the grimness of his expression. 'I was stupid, that's all. I just thought I was born a mermaid instead of a poor human.'

'Is that the truth?' He was still regarding her with that intensely disturbing expression.

'Oh, Kyle,' she whispered with quiet desperation. 'Of course it is.'

'I wasn't sure. That's how you've got me.'

'You're *crazy*!' She felt helpless and agitated. 'I would never do anything so . . . cowardly.'

'You didn't want to marry me again,' he pointed out.

Lynda put up a hand and pushed a few drifting curls off her forehead. 'But you always get what you want.'

'It's the *how*, isn't it?' A shadow of self-contempt passed across his handsome, autocratic dark face.

'You look tired, Kyle.' Almost tentatively she touched his hand. 'Please lie down beside me.'

'Are you sure you trust me?' The fold between his black brows gave him a dangerous look.

'You'll be asleep in five minutes.'

He didn't answer, but looked away, the outline of his profile clear-cut against the golden light.

'*Please*, Kyle.' She gave a harsh little sob. 'I think I need you beside me.'

'There are violet shadows under your eyes. You look very frail.'

'I'm not!' She tried to make a joke of it, realising that beneath his deep tan his skin had a distinct pallor. 'I kept myself afloat until you raced to the rescue.'

'I could have been too late.' His usually vibrant voice was absolutely toneless.

'But you weren't, Kyle. Now please get some rest. This happens to be a very big bed.'

Unexpectedly he smiled and it lit his sombre dark face in a wondrous fashion. 'Just be careful not to ask me in again tomorrow night!'

In the soft, pearly dawn Lynda came awake conscious that a dark head was lying heavily against her breast. She wished it might lie there for ever. Was this her ruthless Kyle? Didn't he realise that in sleep he had turned to her for comfort? Gentle tears slid out of her eyes. She wanted to bring her hand up to caress him, but he had her pinned. Probably her slightest

movement would wake him. There was a slight flush
across his high cheekbone and his black lashes were
very thick and long. He had always been perfect
physically to her. He had always been everything she
wanted. Was she being heartless, condemning him for
a passing infidelity? It happened. Was she supposed to
dry her tears and be a good wife regardless?

She lay wide-eyed for a long time, then eventually
drifted back to sleep. When she awoke again to a
thousand birds' song, Kyle had gone.

The doctor called in again mid-morning and pronounced her all but recovered from her ordeal.

'That was a bad experience, poor child. You're
going to have to listen to Kyle in future.'

'Yes, Doctor.' She smiled at him sweetly. 'I was
only hoping to be able to race him, but then I spoilt
everything.'

'Better put Phil out of his agony,' the doctor
remarked to Kyle. 'I think he was expecting to be shot
at dawn.'

'He's going to get quite a lecture,' Kyle said without
smiling. 'Beginners can't be allowed to go sailboarding
by themselves. Lynda was supposed to be with the
group. He was supposed to be watching the lot of
them.'

'It was my fault, Kyle,' Lynda protested. 'Phil
explained to us all the need for safety-mindedness.'

'He gave you a false idea of yourself,' Kyle corrected
her crisply. 'You're good, but not that good. Even
natural ability has to be backed up by plenty of
experience.'

'And common sense. Please don't be too hard on
him,' she begged. 'He did get a terrible fright.'

Whatever was said to Phil Hunt, Lynda was never

to find out. But at least he wasn't to be dismissed. When she was allowed down on to the beach in the afternoon Phil was out on the water, water-skiing with one of his pupils behind a boat.

'Do you think we could go over to Luana,' she asked dreamily. 'It looks so perfect just by itself.'

'Quite frankly,' Kyle answered dryly, 'I think it's too romantic. The tide's in and most of the boats are out. We could be all alone there.'

'I'm sorry. We can't go?'

'Don't look at me sideways with those smoky-grey eyes!'

'Let's see if we can get a boat.' Lynda lowered her lashes.

'I'll row there if I have to.' He laughed gently in his throat. 'We've had enough romance anyway. I expect everyone feels like that the second time around.'

Of course he had no difficulty getting a boat. One was always kept on standby in case he needed it, and soon they were looking back at Caprice from across the fabulously blue, crystal-clear water.

'Such perfect weather we've had.' Lynda knew her near-disaster of the day before had her emotionally off balance. It could even be said she had done everything today to make herself desirable. She was wearing a brief blue bikini beneath a boldly coloured cover-up that nevertheless marked the cleft between her breasts, her narrow waist and the long golden length of her legs. It was a decidedly eye-catching outfit and it did rather proclaim a total shift in her attitude. It was provocative, and so was she.

The coral islet was quite empty and it couldn't have been lovelier. The brilliant sun shone down on the coral strand with the palest aquamarine water lapping gently at the edge. It was far, far away from the normal world, even the luxuriant beauty of Caprice rising cone-like in the distance. Pandanus palms lined the beach and caring visitors over the years had planted native wild flowers for ground cover, showy little flowers that showed their pink and golden faces to the sun, gardenia-scented white trumpet flowers that bloomed in summer profusion, several species of hibiscus and the almost inde-structible oleanders that glowed in all the apricots, pinks and crimsons.

'Paradise!' Lynda crunched the white sand under her bare toes. 'I like uninhabited islands more than all the others.'

'You sound astonishingly like you used to.' Kyle's densely blue gaze fixed itself on her. She was standing on tiptoe like a dancer with one leg extended and she had picked a huge crimson hibiscus and pushed it through her hair.

'It was yesterday, I think. It shook me up.' The air was so clean and fresh and sweet, like apples mixed up with salt.

'Try asking *me* what it was like,' he said.

'Too complicated.' She wouldn't look at him. 'Just let's enjoy this—the complete isolation. We're strangers.'

'Oh?' He went towards her and she fled.

'We have to be certain of this island, my lord.'

'Then we'll walk all around it. It shouldn't take us long.'

She was a little startled when he caught her up and took her hand, but then she became lost in the old enchantment. Griefs dissolved, the pitiless confi-dences. It was like before, when he had loved and wanted her and each was the stronger for their mutual delight.

When she spoke to point out this or that her voice was the happy, confident one he had once known.

'Oh, look, look. It's a turtle!' She caught his arm and they stood together to watch the slow progress of the huge sea-going green turtle that was everywhere throughout the Barrier Reef waters. This one was at least four feet in length and it had to weigh hundreds of pounds.

'Fancy eating the poor thing!' Lynda shuddered.

'Some people consider them a real delicacy. The eggs too.'

'I'd be quite afraid to eat one. They look like the ancients.'

More time passed. An idyll while the sun travelled across the sky and began to move down on the western horizon. They swam. They lay in the sun. They opened the picnic basket, drank the cold wine and ate a little of the food and some of the delicious grapes. It was a fantasy world and they spoke of lots of things, boats and sailing, variable winds and tides. They spoke of books they had read in the intervening years; films and theatre, a hundred and one easy things, and then they fell silent.

I want him to make love to me, Lynda thought. I want it so badly it was like a delicious dementia.

'Kyle——' She sat up, bending over him so his face and the upper part of his body was in shadow.

'Um?' He didn't open his eyes.

'Do you want me?'

'Of course I do.'

'Please open your eyes.'

'I'm giving you plenty of time to be sure.'

'You mean you're making me beg.'

'That too.' He moved so incredibly swiftly their positions were reversed, his blue eyes blazing with an uninhibited sensuality. 'Is this just a mood, Lynda? We're here where nothing can harm us?'

'It *is* like magic,' she answered.

'And with reality I suppose you'll turn away from me again?'

'I wanted to kiss you this morning.' Her grey eyes were very large and soft.

'Why didn't you?' Already she had released something bitter.

'I was afraid.'

'Of loving. Of being loved. Too badly.'

'Have you ever loved me, Kyle?' she asked seriously.

'You think I've only *made* love to you?' His hand moved up and slid across her breast.

'Did you ever want to know the *real* me?'

'The real you is hard to find. Just fleeting glances.'

She knew what he meant.

'Please talk to me, Lynda,' Kyle said softly.

'I can't when you're caressing me.' Her body arched slightly.

'Will it help if I leave you alone?'

'Oh, *no!*' Her shimmering eyes threatened tears.

'In any case, I can't!'

Now her breasts were exposed to the golden sunlight, the long line of her body, and as he ran his hands over her she cried aloud in longing. 'Why can't there just be the two of us?'

He hesitated a moment as though something had made him uncertain, but the tumult was building inside him too fast.

He lifted her in his arms and carried her to where the wildflowers covered the shadowed dunes, and there he made love to her until her heart shook and she cried out his name over and over again, a high-pitched, seemingly endless little cry that he could only just recall when he came to himself.

CHAPTER SIX

Maybe if their lovemaking had continued that night, Lynda would have come out with her terrible burden, but when they returned to the island the manager was waiting anxiously for them with the gravest of news.

'It's your grandfather, Kyle,' he informed them without delay. 'He collapsed at a meeting this afternoon. It's been diagnosed as a stroke.'

Kyle's face tightened alarmingly and he recoiled from the blow. 'And how *is* he?'

'I believe the exact message was, hanging by a thread.'

'God!'

Lynda said nothing, too appalled to find words and uncertain of the right ones. Sir Neville had never been her friend, but she could not endure to see Kyle so distressed.

'We have the helicopter ready to take you to the mainland where you'll pick up your grandfather's jet,' the manager told them.

'Thank you,' Kyle nodded remotely. 'You'd better send someone up to help us pack.'

'Certainly.' Relieved to be able to do something constructive, the manager signalled another staff member. 'Allow me to say how very sorry we are.'

Still exquisitely in harmony with him, Lynda took Kyle's hand, encouraged beyond words as his fingers curled tightly around hers.

'Despite everything, Lynda,' he said tensely, 'we

have to stay together. It won't be easy. The problems are just beginning.'

In fact they had already begun in earnest, starting with the chaos in the Endfield organisation. It was only when Kyle eventually arrived back at the house that everyone began to settle down.

'Where is he?' Kyle exclaimed at once, while his mother clung desperately to his hands. Lynda was scarcely noticed, at that stage she was much too unimportant, but she noticed any number of things. Kyle's handsome, elegant uncles wore a look of intense strain, the wives were chainsmoking; there were many strangers to her either seated in the living room or pacing through the corridors, Christine was crying in an appalling, uncontrollable fashion, and she was being comforted not by her long-time sympathetic friend, Blair Neale, but by the one person Lynda felt more animosity towards than anyone else in the world—Olivia.

Disaster upon disaster, and as Christine cried and mumbled words incoherently Olivia lifted her dull gold head and staked Lynda with her eyes.

Here I am again! the glance said. You didn't ever think you were going to get rid of me. I'm part of the family and here I am to prove it.

On such a distressing occasion Olivia's long, amber eyes were bright with a peculiar amusement, but if Lynda felt anger and uncertainty she certainly wasn't going to show it. She nodded coolly in Olivia's direction, but as if he sensed she needed his support Kyle turned away from his obviously distraught mother and drew his wife to his side.

'I'm going up to Grandfather, Lynda,' he said rapidly. 'Come with me.'

'But she mustn't!' Anthea cried at once. 'It's *you*

Grandfather has hung on to see!'

'Come, Lynda.' Kyle's arm tightened around his wife's shoulders.

'But, darling, it could upset him,' Anthea beseeched.

'From what you tell me,' Kyle answered gravely, 'Grandfather is beyond upset. Lynda is my wife. We're together.'

Christine, who had been huddled in an armchair, suddenly darted up, throwing back Olivia's protective hand. Her eyes were swollen from weeping and her fair skin was unbecomingly blotched. 'Just how loyal can a man get?' she shrieked. 'We've all been sitting here sick and terrified waiting for you, and you're going to look after your *wife*?'

Her unbalanced glance chilled Lynda to the bone, but Kyle put two hands on his sister's shoulders and grasped them strongly. 'I'm wondering in despair, Christine, when you're ever going to grow up.'

'Oh, don't say that, Kyle,' she begged him. 'You can't sincerely believe Grandfather would want to see Lynda?'

'I'm going to make very sure he sees us together,' Kyle answered very harshly indeed. 'We won't go into your motives for wanting to exclude her. I'm not sure I want to hear them anyway, but if you're looking to keep your brother as your friend, you'd better accept my wife.'

'Exactly!' Anthea looked deeply into her daughter's face, plainly warning her, but Kyle was no longer there to witness it. He and Lynda went quickly up the grand stairway, turned right at the top and hurried along the wide corridor to Sir Neville's private suite of rooms.

Ralph Beresford, Sir Neville's private physician and

long-time friend, was hovering in and out of a doorway, but when he saw Kyle and Lynda he hurried towards them.

'Oh, thank God!' He gave Lynda a quick, acknowledging glance, but spoke to Kyle. 'He won't live until dawn.'

'I can't believe it——'

'Neither can I.' The doctor was obviously groping for composure. 'He's always seemed so invincible, but now the light is going out.'

'Go in first, darling,' Lynda looked up at her husband's tightly closed face, knowing full well the grief that was in him. 'I'll wait until you're ready.'

'Good girl!' Doctor Beresford patted her as much to calm himself as her.

Something in her manner and the way she looked at him seemed to reassure Kyle, for he bent and kissed her cheek then turned and walked through the door into his grandfather's bedroom.

'You've just reached him in time,' Doctor Beresford told Lynda. 'He was determined he wasn't going to die until he'd seen Kyle. Extraordinary, that! He should be dead, but he isn't. He would never have held out for the boys, but he held out for Kyle. He was always the chosen one—Richard's son.'

After perhaps ten minutes Kyle came back very quietly for Lynda, holding out his hand.

'Grandfather can't talk except for his eyes. He's going fast.'

Hand in hand they walked to the edge of the huge bed, and Lynda was stunned to see the man who had indeed looked invincible only a week ago reduced to the waxy frailty of near-death.

The tears spurted to her eyes and one fell on the old man's hand. 'Can he hear me?' she whispered.

'Of course he can.' Kyle's voice was as taut as his body. 'Whatever you've thought, Lynda, Grandfather has always admired you.'

'Yes.' Lynda touched the still, veined hand gently and it seemed once fierce, ice-blue gaze that turned to her was full of light. It was extraordinarily comforting, and as a gesture of her own reconciliation she bent over the old man and kissed him on the temple.

'He nodded,' Kyle said proudly, acknowledging the force of the old man's will.

Sir Neville, pitiably reduced by a massive stroke, had indeed nodded.

'I'll leave you together now.' Lynda walked away quickly and outside in the passageway stumbled into the doctor's waiting arms.

'There, my dear! It's always terrible, these scenes. I can never get used to them, and Neville has been my friend. Kyle is lucky he has you to fill what's going to be a great void in his life. The old man reared him, you know—shaped him. He played a doubly important role, grandfather and father. Neville won't mind if I pay Kyle the compliment. He's everything his grandfather wanted him to be, which is a far better man than my dear old friend claimed to be. Neville knew his failings. He hurt a lot of people all the time, but you'll know far better than I do, Kyle has heart.'

A few moments later Kyle came to the door and at the expression on his face Doctor Beresford hurried in. Lynda herself went to stand at the open doorway, finding it suddenly intolerable what she already knew. Sir Neville was dead.

With typical shrewdness and more than a hint of the old ruthlessness, Sir Neville left a scrupulously detailed will. Sir Neville's sons had long resigned themselves to the knowledge that they would never sit in their father's chair, but both of them had gone up one rung. If the truth were known (and Nick Endfield admitted it freely) they had quite enough power and responsibility as it was, so Kyle, as his grandfather had long intended, reigned supreme.

The greatest shock of the will, in fact the only shock, was Lynda's inclusion. Disliking too much money and thinking it dangerous, Sir Neville had nevertheless moved her up with his granddaughter to a position of wealth—a state of affairs quite a few members of the family seemed to find decidedly odd. Not so Kyle, who had a view of his late grandfather no one else shared.

For the first stunned month when the Endfield empire had to learn to survive without its founder, the household scarcely saw Kyle. His life was one long grind of meetings that seemed to go on from early morning to late at night and often at the weekends. Like his grandfather had been, now he was surrounded by key men and advisers, and occasionally Lynda booked herself an appointment just to see him.

'Just give us a little more time to settle down,' he told her. 'The companies are in good shape, but there are a few changes I'd like to make.'

His uncles, of course, and the cousins who were employed in the various Endfield concerns, remained on the best possible terms with him, and as soon as it was clear that absolutely no disasters were about to happen, everyone began to settle back into a kind of normal life. The papers had run articles tracing Sir Neville Endfield's fifty years of power and they had even resurrected a family photograph of Sir Neville, looking very upright and handsome, standing alongside his grandson and a beautiful, smiling young girl, her dark hair and a little of her face shrouded by a gauzy, flyaway bridal veil. They all looked totally happy, which was a good thing the papers had not popped up at the divorce.

Is that *me*? Lynda thought wistfully. That innocent young girl?

It had been quite impossible to think about setting up house with Kyle so busy presiding over meetings and flying all over the far-flung empire, so all the old, complicated relationships went on. Joel continued to act the opulent playboy as if he didn't know the meaning of the word mourning.

'Mother, *you* may feel enormously sad,' he told Anthea, 'but I feel absolutely nothing at all. Grandfather didn't care two hoots about me and I didn't care about him, and that's it!'

'How can you even bear to say it?' Anthea protested. 'Grandfather loved you. He loved us all.'

Lynda thought it was Christine who muttered: 'Bunk!'

Christine for her part had every intention of continuing hostilities with Lynda—at least on every occasion except the rare one when Kyle was present. As Lynda was beginning to see it, Kyle was the only person in the world Christine seemed able to relate to. Anthea's maternal instinct might well have existed, but it didn't seem to work, at depth, with her daughter. The plain fact of the matter was, Christine was a deep disappointment to her mother. She was neither beautiful nor talented. She had, as Anthea often moaned, 'no conversation'. She had few interests, fewer friends, and a far from winning nature. All she did have was money—so much of it, it flung gold dust in at least a few people's eyes. These were the social climbers who professed to enjoy her caustic tongue and the one true friend who never appeared to abandon her—Olivia. Olivia, it was true, had a pedigree, but it was no secret that her father had invested a good deal of his money in an ambitious real estate project that 'bombed'. To be truly successful now, Olivia *had* to marry money, and as quickly as possible. As strikingly good-looking as she was, Olivia had reached the worrying age of thirty when all the young manhood she could have married were already married off.

'Of course the only guy in the world who's ever meant anything to her is Kyle!' Christine repeated this often to anyone who would listen and equally loudly to those who wouldn't; for instance, Lynda, who always managed to keep her temper under control, Joel, who often retaliated with something rude, and Anthea, Olivia's godmother, who had come to look on her goddaughter differently. It was absolutely over the fence to drag Christine off to a fashion showing and then put half the collection Olivia had picked out for herself on Christine's account.

'It won't *do*, Christine!' Anthea's beautifully modulated voice rang with dismay. 'I'm beginning to think Olivia is just using you.'

'Does it matter?' Christine had replied cynically. 'In fact I get far more of a kick out of being seen with Olivia than caring if she spends my money. What are friends for?'

'I'm not as happy about Olivia as I used to be,' Anthea confided to Lynda in private. 'I've had just about enough of her putting things on Christine's accounts. Obviously with Billy's big scheme gone down the drain, they're all feeling the pinch, but there is such a thing as pride.'

Here's to it! Lynda thought, having abandoned it

for Kyle's bed. No matter what the strain of continuing to live in the family home, Kyle's lengthy, enforced absences, Olivia's hovering on the periphery of their lives, everything was near-meaningless in the light of their continuing lovemaking. It was *their* world—a surreal world. They made love first and talked afterwards. If Lynda ever went to sleep while she was trying to wait up for him, Kyle had only to touch her shoulder and she would move into his arms. He had only to walk into a room and say Hi to her and they were both transported by the need to be together. Often in her solitary daytime world Lynda thought of having a child, a baby that would strengthen their union and add to their joy, but instinctively she knew the time wasn't right. There was only one way they could truly be a family, and that was to find their own home.

'Say, isn't it about time the two of us had lunch?' Lynda dashed out into the hallway to grab Kyle's arm. He had finished off an important phone call rather smartly and now, briefcase in hand, he was heading for the nearest door.

'Great!' he said comfortably.

'You mean it?'

'Oh, yes, I do.' He bent his head and kissed her lingeringly at the corner of her mouth. 'Make it the Sandpiper, one o'clock. I always did like to show you off.'

'I rather fancy luncheon myself,' Anthea said when Lynda told her. 'You and I must make it a day. I'll invite along a few of my friends. Of course, we can't do any entertaining for a few more months, but little get-togethers are in order.'

Lynda dressed for her lunch date with a feeling of pleasurable excitement. She was allowing what had happened before—she was allowing herself to be deeply in love with her husband. What had happened between Kyle and Olivia was in the past. She would never now raise the subject, neither could she allow herself to think, even for a few seconds, that they would ever take up their liaison again.

'Oh, you do look smart!' said Anthea, regarding her daughter-in-law's immaculate appearance with obvious pleasure. 'I'm glad you're seeing life differently these days, Lynda. Really, you've become amazingly mature!'

You mean I'm older and wiser, Lynda thought. More able to bear the frustrations. And one was just ahead for her.

Out in the entrance hall the phone rang, and even as Lynda went to answer it, her skin began to pale.

It was Kyle, and as she went on holding the phone tightly he told her he was very sorry but he couldn't possibly get away.

'That's all right,' she said.

He sighed, she thought with relief.

'I'll make it up to you, darling!' His voice was dynamic, very businesslike.

'Lunches are for other people,' she assured him.

'Don't sit at home,' he told her. 'Keep the appointment. Take Anthea.'

'I'll be okay.' Lynda tried to cling to a little of her former buoyant mood. 'What time should we expect you home this evening?'

'God knows!' he groaned. 'There's not the remotest chance before seven.'

Anthea was still turning the glossy pages of the *Architectural Digest*. 'So who was that?'

'Kyle.' Lynda tried to keep her voice bright. 'He can't make it.'

'To be quite frank, my dear, I didn't think he could. Don't forget I've been through all this myself.'

'Yes, of course you have.' Lynda stared off into the middle distance, thinking what Anthea's life might have been like.

'So what are you going to do?' Anthea asked quite kindly. 'I'd come with you, only it takes me ages to dress.'

'Well, seeing *I'm* dressed. I'll go into town anyway. There are a few things I have to do.'

Mercifully Anthea didn't ask, like what?

Could she possibly sit through a solitary luncheon? Not really. After all, she wasn't hungry now. Unlike Anthea or even Olivia, both compulsive shoppers, she felt downright uncomfortable with excessive self-indulgence, so calling in on Anthea's exclusive haunts was definitely out. What she really needed to do was find a job or get heavily involved in charity work. Not being a natural-born lady of leisure was placing her in a small dilemma. She had to find something to gainfully employ her time. There were far better things to do in the world than to sit still and look pretty. She needed work, and now she had hours to kill.

Finally she decided on having lunch on her own. She hadn't called and cancelled the booking in any case, so she was fairly well compelled to go. Maybe the waiter could find her some secluded little nook so she could sit back and watch the river and concentrate on the ferry that plied people to and fro.

Shortly before one o'clock, Lynda parked the Daimler lovingly, still wishing over and over that Kyle had been there to meet her. The big white building behind her, perched on the cliff like a seagull, bore the name SANDPIPER, and Lynda drew a deep breath and walked right in. No need to be nervous or apologetic. It was perfectly permissible for a woman to eat alone.

A tall man was just ahead of her and coming up the stairs Lynda realised with a touch of shock that it was Scott.

Lord! She had the wildest impulse to run down the stairs again, but he turned with the faint smile of fellow-diners that immediately hardened into a mutual dismay.

'Lynda!'

'What a surprise, Scott! How are you?'

'Fine. Fine.' He said it awkwardly, frowning instead of smiling. 'Are you meeting someone?'

She relaxed then and gave a rueful smile. 'Actually I've been stood up. I was having lunch with Kyle, but at the last minute he couldn't get away.'

'So now you're on your own?'

'Exactly. I'm going to hide in a corner.'

'Not at all.' Scott's own manner eased. 'You're having lunch with me. You'll be doing me a great favour. My own colleague had to pull out at the last moment. Sometimes it's impossible to make rendez-vous in business.'

'That will be nice, Scott,' Lynda said simply.

So now they had the best table, which had been originally set aside for Mr Kyle Endfield.

'So how are you?' Scott asked, after they had ordered. That had been a bad moment out on the stairs, but now he had calmed his agitated heart.

'Well, Scott.'

'Happy?'

'I think I probably am.'

'Only think it?' Scott was thinking with absolute conviction that he would remain a bachelor all his life.

'There are always difficulties, Scott,' she told him.

'You look beautiful,' he said deeply.

'Thank you.' She smiled at him. 'It's always delightful to be told that.'

'Your husband must tell you all the time.'

He looked momentarily so bleak and unhappy Lynda placed a cool hand over his. 'I very much valued our friendship, Scott. All my thoughts of you are good.'

'In a strange way that makes me happier,' he told her ruefully.

'I hope so.' Her fingers tightened.

'Keep doing that, Lynda, and you'll have my pulses racing.'

'Forget me, Scott,' she said softly.

'I regret I can't do that.'

'You *can*.'

'No, my dear.' He lifted his clear eyes. 'Love is a kind of madness, isn't it? There's no shame in loving you. The only shame would be in trying to do something about it.'

'So let's be friends.'

'With your husband such a jealous man?' Scott gave a dry little laugh.

'Kyle's not jealous.' Lynda shook her dark head.

'My dearest child, you can't believe that. Don't forget, I've seen him with murder in his eyes.'

'Blue eyes have twice as much impact when they're blazing.'

'My God, they *do*!' Scott was still remembering. 'You would be incredibly foolish to think your husband would tolerate a close male friend in your life.'

Lynda's smoky eyes flashed. 'My husband can't stop me from having friends of either sex.'

'It wouldn't be the easiest thing for a man to be *your* friend, Lynda. You're a very desirable woman.'

'But surely sex isn't all men think about?' Lynda muttered quietly. Why couldn't a woman have male friends without complications? She needed friends, and she had always felt very secure and comfortable with Scott. Moreover, he was a man of integrity though it was true he was easy to scare.

'But of course it isn't!' Scott was saying very earnestly. 'It's only the first thing.'

'And the last,' Lynda managed to say calmly, and they both laughed—genuine amusement that lightened their faces and brightened their eyes.

'So how is business?' Lynda asked dutifully, getting off the subject.

'Business is good, as usual, but I certainly miss you,' Scott told her. 'You had the uncanny knack of reading my mind. It certainly simplifies things. My secretary right now is a good girl, but she lacks your professionalism. Also she never smiles at me when she walks into the office.'

'You smile at her first and she might catch on.'

'For a while there it was hell,' Scott said, looking away from her lovely face and out of the window. 'At my stage of life I never expected to be so unhappy. For that matter, I never expected to fall in love.'

'There could be someone else waiting for you, Scott. Right now. You have a lot to offer.'

'I'm too quiet and reserved. Sometimes I think I could have won you if I had the nature to sweep you off your feet.' He gave her his quiet, charming smile. 'Your husband is the kind of man to do that. He's a man of action and from all I hear, he's set to write business history. One would have thought his grandfather's death would have caused a few tremors, but instead it's the word that Endfield is up and away.'

'Kyle was terribly upset,' Lynda said quietly, and sipped at her wine. 'He was closer to Sir Neville than anyone else in the world.'

'I should think his uncles would have resented that bitterly.'

'I beg your pardon, sir, madam——' The waiter arrived with their seafood entrée, crab croquettes served with tartare sauce and lemon wedges, and set the dishes down before them.

'Thank you. That looks good,' Lynda said.

Scott sat back until the waiter had departed. 'It's very unusual to set a young man over the older directors' heads.'

'They weren't hurt by it, Scott,' Lynda hastened to assure him. 'It would be very difficult not to give Kyle his due. He *is* the man for the job, and that was the only reason it was given to him.'

'For sure,' Scott agreed rather dryly. 'Obviously his grandfather wouldn't have cared about him at all if he hadn't been brilliant. I don't understand that kind of man. The rest of them mustn't have had a pleasant time. It would be difficult for the younger brother to function well when he's inevitably outshone at every turn.'

'You can hardly blame Kyle for being successful,' Lynda said with faint reproach. 'Joel could have chosen any career he liked. He didn't *have* to go into the business. There was no pressure on him to do that.'

'Surely it was hoped he would take his place?' Scott said sceptically. 'I mean, it's a vast organisation. They're in everything!'

'Joel doesn't have to work. That's his tragedy.'

'And Martin?' Scott put down his fork and looked

across at her searchingly. 'I hear he's been transferred to the backblocks?'

'To see how he works out.'

'Is that all?' Scott asked abruptly.

'Why, of course, yes.' Lynda hoped her gaze was clear and unflinching.

'Forgive me, my dear, but I know you were worried about him.'

'Well, that's all over.' With false calm Lynda returned her eyes to her plate. 'He writes to me about every fortnight.'

'But he's given no opportunity to come home.'

'A toughening up process,' Lynda explained. 'Kyle thinks Martin needs more effort to succeed.'

'That's certainly true!' Scott presumed to agree. 'Once I had the crazy idea you were being forced into remarrying Endfield through your brother.'

'Good heavens, Scott!' Lynda murmured in a voice that said don't be ridiculous, when in reality she was riveted to her chair.

'You're denying it, then?' Scott drained his glass.

'But how incredible, Scott?'

'I beg your pardon, my dear—not incredible at all. Shortly after you'd spoken to me of your worries—*too* shortly, I recall, you asked me to accept your immediate resignation. I'm convinced you didn't want to marry Endfield. You *had* to.'

'Really, Scott!' Lynda pushed aside her plate.

'You've gone pale,' he said anxiously. 'I'm sorry.'

He had grasped her hand so firmly she couldn't release it. 'I'm shocked by what you're saying.'

'And the very thought of it has nearly driven me insane!'

Diners were streaming past them, but Scott was too far gone to notice. The whole matter of Lynda's hasty marriage had been preying on his brain.

'Why, hello there!' A woman's exquisitely mocking voice interrupted their rather bitter conversation. 'Surely you're not out, Lynda, on an illicit luncheon date?'

Scott, bewildered and embarrassed, rose to his feet and Lynda looked up into Olivia's sparkling, jeering eyes. Her friends had gone ahead, but Olivia was clearly sticking around for her little bit of fun.

'How are you, Olivia?' Lynda didn't smile. 'You know Scott, of course.'

'Of *course*!' There was another wave of amused mockery on Olivia's smooth, good-looking face. 'I didn't realise you two were seeing each other again?'

The bitch! Scott thought, shocked. 'I'm terribly sorry to disappoint you, Miss Dowling,' he said pleasantly, taking the offensive into his own hands, 'but Lynda and I met quite by chance—a very happy chance as far as I'm concerned.'

'But how extraordinary!' Olivia looked back at him with smiling dislike. 'You looked rather alarmingly unhappy to me—and how could anyone explain to Kyle that you were holding his wife's hand?'

'At least we're sure *you* will have a try,' Lynda replied scathingly, her grey eyes very large and brilliant. 'Don't let us keep you.'

'That's quite all right!' Olivia trilled. 'I'm always on the lookout for news.'

'There's no doubt about that.' Scott sat down again, angry and upset. 'What a terrible woman! I should think she's caused a great deal of trouble in her time.'

Olivia was now seated at her table and whatever she said to her companions had them all turning to look at Lynda in amazement.

'My goodness, what do you suppose she's saying?' Scott asked hoarsely.

'Who cares?' Lynda shrugged philosophically. 'I wouldn't worry too much about it, Scott.'

'I'm not so much worried about myself as you.'

'Kyle's not Henry the Eighth,' she assured him. 'He can't cut off my head at any time.'

Scott looked back at her helplessly. 'But he could give you a bad time.'

'What on earth *for*?' Lynda eyed him rather sharply. 'This is a perfectly innocent meeting in an obviously public place.'

'I was holding your hand,' Scott pointed out wryly.

'Please, Scott!' She tried to speak humorously. 'Don't expect to be torn limb from limb for it.'

'It never takes much to start trouble,' Scott said morosely. 'The best advice I can offer you is tell your husband before that . . . witch gets a chance to.'

Lynda knew the minute she met Kyle's glittery glance that something was wrong. She was folding away clothes in the bedroom and her greeting trailed off at his insufferably formidable expression. Why, in a few years' time he would have all Sir Neville's intimidating demeanour and more!

'You took a bit of a risk today, didn't you?' he asked her precisely.

'You mean driving the Daimler?' She raised her beautifully defined brows.

'Meeting Walker,' he answered, quietly and distinctly.

'I wouldn't say it was risky.' She kept her face and her voice cool, but she had refolded her pink nightgown several times.

'I've got to admit you like danger.'

'In any case, *you* couldn't turn up.' When she should have been explaining the situation quietly and reasonably as it happened, a quick anger was overriding her common sense.

'Did you ring him?' Kyle asked.

'Ring him?' She gave a wild little laugh. 'Do you think I ring other men when the fancy takes me?'

'I would say you might have decided you were going to suit yourself.'

'And why shouldn't I?' She moved to the beautiful antique chest of drawers and carefully folded away the pile of filmy garments.

'Look at me, Lynda.' He followed her and gripped her shoulders hard.

'Why?' She spun angrily, looking up into his sapphire, slitted eyes. 'Surely I don't have to check with you if I want to speak to an old friend?'

'But he *isn't* an old friend,' he shook her. 'He wanted to marry you.'

'When I no longer had a choice.'

'Come on now,' he said cruelly, 'who have I been making love to all these weeks? I can't wait to get home to you, and you've definitely been willing.'

'So my body has a life of its own?' she retaliated unwisely.

'Is that what it is?'

'You're nearly crushing my bones!' Lynda complained.

'I'd like that.' He looked down at her, rather pale and fragile-looking in an ivory silk robe.

'Olivia rang you, didn't she?' Lynda asked bitterly.

'I must ask my secretary not to let her through.'

'Really?' Her smoky eyes were huge. 'I thought she might have been your paid informant.'

'Olivia is the biggest bitch imaginable,' Kyle said harshly.

'So you've finally found out!' She wanted to fling herself into his arms, instead she thudded her small fist into his chest. 'Bitch or not, you swallow every word she tells you.'

'I know Walker,' he said deadly quietly. 'I know he's in love with you. Aren't you afraid of that, or do you want it?'

'You astonish me, Kyle,' she said, breathless and trembling.

'Of course I do. I have every intention of holding on to my wife.'

'But I met Scott quite by chance.'

'You didn't contact him at all?'

'No, damn it, I *didn't*!'

'All right, I believe you.'

'And a great big thanks for *nothing*!'

'Why are you so angry?' He caught her to him.

'Why are *you*?' she retorted.

'You're the one who ran off the last time.' His eyes were one furious blue blaze. 'It doesn't exactly make a man feel secure.'

'Kyle Endfield not secure?' she said incredulously. 'I don't think I care for the sound of that.'

'I'm not going to fight with you, Lynda,' he said.

'Who's fighting? No one, I hope.' Her eyes large and brilliant flashed upwards.

'You're in a strange mood.' Forcibly he held her chin.

'I was perfectly all right until you arrived home,' she said tautly. 'Olivia rings you in her usual perfectly hateful manner and you race home to play the dictator.'

'And why not? Another divorce would be catastrophic.'

'Is that supposed to be funny?' Suddenly she was crying.

'Lynda, *don't*!' he begged.

'Let me go!' She lifted her hand and swung it wildly. 'You *are* a dictator, Kyle.'

'What the hell else can I be, with my way of life? Don't you ever feel a grain of sympathy for the kind of days I have to get through? Don't you think I *want* to meet you for lunch? Go to the sea or the mountains? Enjoy my wife? I do, but my life has been heavily involved since the day I was born. I just opened my eyes and found myself rich. I can't get rid of it as fast as I can like the rest of the family. I have the responsibility to hold intact all my grandfather and my father worked so hard for. I'm going to hold it for my son.'

'And what about *your* son's mother?' Lynda demanded.

'That's why I'm going to make this work.' Harshness returned to his voice. 'Forgive me if I've made you angry, but you know how people talk. Everybody in our world knows all about our off-and-on-again marriage.'

'Do they know it was on again by way of revenge?'

Sudden anger flared in his blue eyes. 'I was prepared to do anything I had to do to get you back. As I am to hold you.'

The words hung in the air with the heaviness of a warning. 'I don't know why you want me, Kyle.' Her deep-seated doubts and uncertainties were reflected in her face.

'I fell in love with you the moment I saw you,' he said, with no tenderness or even feeling in his dark voice. 'It *had* to be you, then and now. I'm very one-track about the things I want even when they don't want me.'

'I've never *said* that.' She put the back of her hand to her mouth like a small, shocked child. 'When have I ever done anything, that you should come home so mistrustful? Trust is all-important, isn't it?'

'I don't think I'm ever going to forget you left me.' His eyes reflected a terrible bitterness.

'But I had to,' she said urgently, her flawless skin burning with colour.

'I know that,' his reaction came without warning, 'What I don't know is—why?'

The chandelier above them seemed to rock crazily and as her eyes fluttered closed he picked her up with crushing strength and carried her over to the wide bed.

'This isn't solving anything, Kyle,' she said distractedly, trying to bury her silky dark head in the pillows, seeking not to cry.

'No.' Even he took a deep, ragged breath. 'But it's all we've got.'

'Ah, yes.' She raised her hand to cover the pain in her eyes.

For a moment he looked down at her vulnerable, melancholy young beauty, then with a muffled groan he lifted the upper part of her body and stripped off her robe.

'*This* is what I've wanted all day,' he muttered with a touch of self-contempt.

She still hid her eyes. 'It just happened you had a million other things to do.'

'What's more, I'll always have them!' He spoke with brutal finality, but the hands that shaped her breasts had the sensitivity of a master.

'O—o—*oh*!' A gasping little cry escaped her, a struggle against ecstasy.

'I know your body better than you do yourself,' he

told her deeply. How could she deny it? His power over her was so complete, so inexhaustible she was wise to go in fear of it. 'But your brain, Lynda,' Kyle gave a harsh little laugh. 'That's far too complex.'

Was she the only one capable of complexity? How could he make love to her so passionately and then turn away to Olivia or another woman like her? Brief encounters that were nevertheless the driving force in wrecked marriages.

His hands moved down her body, drenching her in heat. 'Tell me you want me,' he said in a soft rasp.

'*Oh!*'

'Maddening, isn't it? Enough to drive you crazy.'

Suddenly Lynda opened her eyes, expecting to see his handsome face glittery with triumph, instead his expression was wretched as though underneath all that authority he was as desperate and vulnerable as she was.

'Come to me,' she said shakily, and her beautiful grey eyes filled with tears. 'You don't need me to tell you I want you.'

He made no answer but lowered his head, thoroughly silencing her mouth.

They had made love for a long time, but never once did either of them say those beautiful words: I love you. Lynda wanted to cry it out spontaneously even as she did the half-inarticulate endearments, but her total abandonment would have been far too costly. Once she had whispered, even shouted with the joy of it, 'I love you, Kyle!' but as soon as he was sure of her he would turn to another woman for diversion. Maybe the urge was already upon him. Olivia was still the same, still there and still coveting. A lot of men were attracted to persistent women. Did she really dare to think she could hold Kyle exclusively? The most beautiful, the most fascinating women in the world had written of their anguish when confronted with rivals. Depending on their temperament, culture, circumstances, many had been forced to turn a blind eye to infidelity, but Lynda knew she didn't have the special qualities to survive anything so serious as a husband's 'frailties'. If no other man existed for her as a lover, why couldn't she expect the same allegiance of Kyle?

Hours later she went over the same thing in her mind, but eventually she came back to the old, nagging worry. Maybe it was as they said, love was a woman's whole life but only a passing excitement for a man. Quite certainly Kyle didn't really believe that he had deceived her with Olivia; the idea of even breaking up their marriage hadn't entered his mind. So it seemed she was expected to tolerate his occasional strayings in exchange for what other women would have thought a great deal. Unfortunately, because she loved him, indeed he meant everything to her, any kind of pretence was a torment. What didn't seem to matter to him at all had made her a victim of the divorce courts. This time she had sworn to stay with him, but nothing else.

CHAPTER SEVEN

'GOOD morning, Mother, girls!' Joel walked breezily through the open sliding glass doors and out on to the secluded rear terrace. Here sunlight fell in brilliant chinks through a magnificent pergola hung with a grapevine heavy with fruit. Beyond was a huge, informal entertainment area complete with a specially designed swimming pool, more like an emerald lagoon surrounded by a summer-flowering annuals than the usual rectangle, but what was particularly beautiful were the domed-shaped hills they looked up to. Anthea liked to have breakfast on the rear terrace for much of the year, and if it caused Mrs Miller the housekeeper and Sarah, her offsider, a good deal more work then surely they were being well paid for it.

'Not going in to the office today, darling?' Anthea asked in the voice of a woman who long since knew the answer.

'They won't miss me.' Joel poured himself fresh pineapple juice but told Sarah to give him 'the works'. This meant sausages, bacon, eggs, a couple of slices of grilled tomato, piping hot toast.

'God knows where you put it all,' Christine said resentfully. Neither of her brothers carried an ounce of superfluous weight, but Christine's life was one long battle against plumpness.

'Pale this morning, aren't we, darling?' Joel sat down beside Lynda and gave her a long, insolent stare.

'You and Kyle thinking of starting a family?'

'Certainly not until we're in our own home,' Lynda returned coolly.

'Still holding out for that one?' Joel leaned back while Sarah set his laden plate down before him.

'Not holding out, just biding my time.' A little maturity was making her almost impervious to Joel's attacks.

'I don't know why you just can't settle,' Christine said angrily. 'How can you possibly expect Kyle to go off and abandon us?'

'Yes,' Joel laughed bitterly. 'After all, we're a pretty immature family. We just can't function without Kyle to look after us.'

'I think you've been using Kyle too long,' Lynda said quietly. 'Think of it as over-exacting payments when Kyle doesn't actually owe you anything.'

'But that's *awful*, dear!' Anthea protested. 'Is it so wrong of us to depend on Kyle?'

'You'd find it quite easy to run this household yourself, Anthea,' Lynda said reasonably. 'You must understand my position. Marriage is a commitment to one another, not to whole families. Kyle and I need a house of our own. We need total privacy and I need to function as mistress of my own home. Surely you recognise my right?'

'Yes, I do,' Anthea said bleakly. 'In fact, my dear, to show you just how much I recognise your dilemma you could draw on my own case history. All my life I've done exactly as I was told. I can't even blame it on being alone, a widow. I knuckled under even as a young bride. This family, as you say, are very good at exacting payments. Grandfather argued that he needed Richard so badly he would build a very big house and we would all live in it. Of course he pressured us dreadfully, especially me, and I allowed him to override us on a most important decision. Being the wife of a rich man and the daughter-in-law of an even richer one took all the work out of everything. I've had nothing in my life but emotional attachments. No decisions, responsibilities, problems to solve. That was all done for me, first by my husband and then by my father-in-law. My sole purpose in life has been to provide children and look good. I didn't even have to rear them. Grandfather took Kyle over and put my other two children down on every occasion.'

'Oh, *please*, Anthea!' Lynda was feeling the older woman's distress.

'Of course it was another generation, you under-stand. Young people have come a long way. Young women have become more independent, secure, though basically, I suppose, we women will always tend to form stronger emotional attachments than men. A career means much more to a man than a woman. They can even live for it, and not a great many women can do that. But I was utterly subservient to my man—I realise this now, more than ever since you've been in our life. You started to fight for your rights from day one. Grandfather told me on a dozen occasions you would soon learn your lesson, but you never did.'

'She couldn't pull her marriage off,' Joel said quickly. 'It failed, or don't you remember?'

'And *we* failed her!' Anthea silenced her son convincingly. 'Worse, we failed Kyle.'

'But we thought we were doing the right thing!' A hot blaze of colour was suffusing Christine's cheeks. 'Who was Lynda to come into the house and start throwing her weight around? Tangling with Grandfather?'

'Standing up to him when we were total cowards,' Joel muttered unexpectedly. 'Funny how we could never get along with Grandfather, yet when we were kids he did try. I suppose he kept hoping I was going to turn into something, but whatever benign god made Kyle what he was forgot about me.'

'*And* me!' Christine spoke with an angry look on her face. 'The only thing I could do was graduate as a Cordon Bleu.'

'Which, to my way of thinking, is a very great deal.' Lynda returned the angry glance. 'In your position, I would have turned it to account.'

'Oh, really?' Christine said sneeringly. 'How? Don't forget Emily was trained in London and Paris. She worked for top restaurants before Grandfather offered her a job. Who needs me with Emily around—and I can't even taste anything without putting on half a stone!'

'That's an exaggeration, dear,' Anthea said mildly. 'And now that Grandfather has gone I'm sure Emily will let you into the kitchen any time you like.'

'That's hardly what I mean,' Lynda said quietly, though she scarcely thought she would get through to Christine who had always bitterly resented her. 'You're a graduate of the Cordon Bleu School of Cookery in London, isn't that right?'

'I have the diploma to prove it.'

'Then why don't you tack it up some place? Open a cookery school of your own? A shop, if you like, selling all the very best in cooking utensils, equipment, whatever. You have the money to do it. You have the skills.'

Christine, for her part, looked absolutely floored. Even her mouth was a rounded O.

'I wouldn't dream of putting our Chris behind a counter,' Joel drawled. 'She's never let herself be halfway nice to anyone. Except maybe Olivia, who cultivates everyone for purposes of her own.'

'Anyway, when you marry Blair you'll come into your own,' Anthea murmured soothingly.

'What if I don't want to marry Blair?' Christine asked her mother sharply. 'All you can think of is marrying me off!'

'Christine, for heaven's sake!'

'I think it would be a great kindness to some poor devil to encourage her to remain a sharp-tongued spinster,' Joel set his knife and fork down and shrugged. 'Let's face it, kiddo, we're write-offs.'

'I seem to remember Kenny Rosewall saying you and Kyle could have made world class tennis players,' Lynda turned her head to face him. 'Whatever happened to that?'

'God, Lynda, I'm terrified of you,' Joel muttered, indeed looking perturbed. 'I didn't need to make my fortune, darling. It was all made for me.'

'Everyone needs to have some pride in himself.'

'Great, the little do-gooder. I love her.'

'It's a pity, that's all.' Lynda shook her head. 'So much promise to come to nothing.'

'Okay, okay,' Joel exclaimed angrily. 'So I could play tennis? So what? Kyle could beat me.'

'Not *every* time,' Christine said suddenly.

'Oh, hell, just about every time,' Joel muttered moodily. 'Anyway, what does it matter? I just enjoyed doing something well.'

'You did a lot of things well,' Anthea said. 'The tragedy was, Kyle always seemed to do them better. Somewhere along the line, you gave up the struggle. I always thought you would have been different had your father lived. Kyle was a magnificent older brother, but no brother can serve as a father. Richard would never have allowed you to give up, and Grandfather's dominating ways were rather destructive.'

'The kiss of death on ambition,' Joel said wryly. 'Grandfather saw tennis as a "jolly good game", not a possible career for one of his grandsons. Anyway, it's much too late now to talk about it. I'm an old man of thirty.'

Because she had always felt a sympathy for him, Lynda persisted where once she would have stopped. 'You're a young man with plenty of money at your disposal. Having plenty of money surely entails responsibilities, moral obligations?'

'We *do* give a great deal to various charitable institutions, Lynda,' Anthea pointed out, with a flash of her still brilliant blue eyes.

'I know that, Anthea,' Lynda tried a fresh start. 'If I seem to be suggesting things, it's only because I'd sincerely like to help. No one can deny you all depend on Kyle very heavily for emotional support. Christine and Joel have just spoken of their inner dissatisfaction, and quite frankly I'm wondering what I'm going to do myself. In fact I've drawn up a list of possibilities I'm going to discuss with Kyle. We all have to find something rewarding in our lives, otherwise the years will stretch into a desert. I believe Christine could and should use her skills to make herself and a lot of other people happier. The same with Joel. There are a lot of kids out there waiting for a direction. Now that I think about it, I can't really see why Joel can't start up a tennis centre or a sporting complex. He's a natural at squash as well as tennis. Add on a fitness centre if you like. People are becoming increasingly interested in keeping fit.'

'But what an extraordinary idea!' Anthea exclaimed.

'*Why?*' Christine and Joel answered together, disappointment in their mother showing on their faces.

'Well . . .' Anthea looked taken aback, 'it just struck me as rather odd. Joel coaching *tennis*?'

'You don't feel I could do it, Mother?' Joel asked ironically.

'I don't feel you would want to do it *long*, dear.'

'Maybe you don't know my true self.' Joel's eyes were bleak. 'You might not believe this, Lynda, but once I had much the same idea, but I was frightened of rocking the boat. I was frequently frightened when Grandfather was alive. Maybe I need some psychiatric treatment.'

'More importantly, Joel,' Lynda reached out and gripped his wrist, 'you need to be your own man. You've got so much more than other people—I don't mean materially, which has been more of a handicap up to date, yet you sometimes speak of yourself as though you were worthless or helpless to alter your own fate. Sir Neville, with the exception of Kyle, has held you all in thrall, but he's not here any more. No one is going to criticise you if you try. Personally I think you could make a positive success of it. You're a great player, and if you want someone else to bolster the centre's prestige, Jake Petersen is home at last and available.'

'My God, so he is!' Joel's expression changed to one of alarmed comprehension. 'Maybe he's thinking of starting up himself. He must have made a lot of money.'

'Maybe he wants a partner?'

Joel nearly hurled himself from the chair. 'I'm going to ring him.'

'Oh, think about this, darling,' Anthea cried distractedly, as if somewhere deep within her she had no confidence in Joel either.

'Let him go, Mother.' Christine, never close to her younger brother, nevertheless spoke up aggressively. 'Joel isn't entirely a fool, you know. What's wrong with his teaching tennis? Teaching is a fine profession, not a cause for contempt. Haven't you noticed the only time Joel likes himself is when he's on a tennis court or a squash court? He can beat just about anyone there. And strangely enough he's good with kids. Remember little Michael Campbell? Joel was endlessly patient trying to help him learn the game.'

'I thought that was because the Campbells were our guests,' Anthea said morosely. 'I mean, he was trying to please Grandfather. *That* was his motivation.'

'You're wrong, Mother,' Christine said wearily. 'Joel was really trying to help the kid. He saw he had natural ability but he had to be shown how. You might recall too, Michael rang us back about six months later to tell us he'd made one of the school teams. He sounded as though he gave Joel all the credit for that.'

'What's worrying you, Anthea?' Lynda asked gently, seeing how Anthea had almost slumped in her chair.

'Joel is so *inconsistent*,' Anthea said worriedly. 'He may work well one day, then the next he'll go off to the races. He hasn't got Kyle's tremendous application or even his energy. He might want to do something positive one day then the next he'll let everyone down. He's been doing that for years, you know. No wonder I'm mistrustful of his handling of his own business.'

'Then let him crash,' Christine said in a caustic voice. 'You know, Mother, there's a lot to be said for the old sink or swim. I suppose I'm unsure about Joel as well, but I believe he needs his chance. He's never wanted to do the same things as Kyle or Grandfather, and up to date his role has been the playboy, ineffectual brother. Let him try to get himself together. Who knows, he may succeed. It would be a heady feeling to actually achieve something. Take Lynda's idea about me, for instance. There's some sense in it. I'll speak to Olivia about it. She usually gives me good advice.'

'If she does, it's news to me!' Anthea said shortly. 'I don't want to turn you against Olivia now. After all, she's my own goddaughter, but her faults are becoming more apparent as she gets older. She's really not terribly truthful either. She's had a few disturbing things to say to me and I surprised her somewhat by challenging her point blank.'

'About what?' Christine looked at her mother wonderingly.

'About people she ran into,' Anthea said evasively. 'Olivia has the peculiar knack of making two and two add up to five.'

'She does exaggerate a little.' Christine stood up quickly to forestall any more of her mother's adverse comments. 'I'll really think about what you said, Lynda. I doubt it could transform me into a happy person, but I do know I can't coast along any longer.'

'But you're going to marry Blair!' Anthea looked up at her daughter with worried, intensely blue eyes.

'No, Mother,' Christine shook her head sadly. 'Blair is a good friend, but I don't love him. I don't think he loves me either. It was just Grandfather's idea and a fairly comfortable way to get rid of me. If and when I marry, I'm going to hope for a man who's as crazy about me as Kyle is about Lynda.'

'You believe that?' The words burst out of Lynda, swift and unbidden.

Christine frowned heavily. 'In fact I think I've done a lot of things to be ashamed of.'

'Christine dear——' Anthea half rose from her chair to try to detain her fleeing daughter. 'Wasn't she crying?' she demanded of Lynda.

'I don't think so.' Lynda too had caught the shimmer of tears. 'In any case, I think it's better to leave her alone.'

'She's always held herself aloof from me,' Anthea wailed. 'Except that I've produced Kyle, you might as well say I'm a failure.'

The same evening Kyle and Lynda had an important dinner appointment, and just as she was finishing dressing Kyle reached over her shoulder and placed a long velvet box on the dressing table. 'Let me see how it looks.'

'It looks very interesting,' she admitted.

'You'll work the extra magic.' Her blue-eyed sorcerer stared at her, arrestingly handsome and elegant in his dinner clothes. 'Is something wrong with the catch?'

'No.' Lynda gave a husky laugh. 'I'm trying to summon up the nerve to open it.'

'Then we'll open it together.' He bent over her, seated as she was at the dressing table, and released the catch on the midnight-blue velvet case.

'Oh, how beautiful!' Lynda heard her own voice, soft and wondering like a little girl's.

'It's about time I gave my wife a present.'

'Another present.'

'Do you wonder I want to?' He took the sapphire and diamond necklace from her nerveless fingers.

'When I think of you it's always pearls and moonstones, but this will match your ring.'

'It's beautiful, Kyle.' She sat there rapt, while he slid the glittering necklace around her neck.

'M'm, it suits you.' He cupped her bare shoulders and stared into the mirror at her reflection. She was wearing white chiffon, closely moulded to the hip, then flaring out into a full skirt, and her light golden tan and the purity of her dress provided a magnificent foil for the exquisitely styled necklace. The sapphires, and there had to be twenty or more of them, had the same remarkable beauty and depth of colour as her ring and like the ring were surrounded by diamonds, each jewelled flower linked by a long leaf-shaped diamond. It was unmistakably an important piece, and Lynda was too much a woman not to appreciate how beautiful it looked on her.

As for Kyle, he stood there watching her intently, his lean, beautifully shaped hands unmoving on her shoulders. 'Do you think you can manage to thank me?'

'Thank you.' She tipped back her head, offering him her glowing mouth.

'Is that an act of martyrdom?' he asked her dryly, letting his hands slip down from her shoulders to the contours of her small but well defined breasts.

'Well, I'm not sure I can handle a love scene right now. We're dressed to go out.'

'More's the pity!' There was a look of controlled sensuality on his face. 'It will be impossible to make an early night of it too.'

'There is a solution,' she told him. 'Ring up and say we're not coming.'

'I'd love to, but I'm afraid we'd be very sadly missed.'

'In any case we might even enjoy it.' Lynda came gracefully to her feet. 'Shall I wear this glorious thing tonight?'

'You can even wear it in bed.' Kyle gave her a brief glance that sizzled along her quickened nerves. 'I'll get your earrings out of the safe.'

She whirled quickly, the outline of her body silhouetted through the floating chiffon. 'You kept them?'

His voice came back, sounding crisp and decisive. 'Sure. They reminded me of the days when I was obsessed by a female.'

'And those days are over?' She knew she had sighed.

'Why don't *you* tell me about it?' he challenged her. 'But you don't say a word, Lynda. Never a word.'

She was standing in the entrance hall waiting for Kyle to join her when Joel came rushing up the broad flight of stairs and into the brilliant flood of light.

'My God!' he exclaimed theatrically, 'a vision!'

'Like it?' Instead of being cool with him, she tried a pirouette and a smile.

'Darling, you're the most beautiful girl in the world!' He moved quickly and caught her into a definitely caressing embrace. 'I want to tell you some good news, and you're responsible for it.'

'Well, tell me?' As with Kyle, she had to tilt her head back to look up to him.

'Jake Petersen and I have been talking for most of the day. I've just come from Jake's place now.'

'And he's interested?'

'Much better!' Joel had lost his languid drawl and replaced it with boyish enthusiasm. 'He's sold on the idea. On his own, with what we have in mind, he'd be under-capitalised, but with me for a partner his ideas have moved into another dimension. Tomorrow we're going to look out some land. Jake knows all about zoning and permits and that kind of thing. To tell you the truth, he's as excited as I am. As an ex-champion he's had plenty of overseas offers to coach, but he loves his own country and he and I are going to provide the champions of the future. The best thing of all, he accepted me just like that. Not because my name is Endfield, though I guess it helped, but because I'm a damn good player and I love the game.'

'I know you do, Joel,' Lynda said softly. 'I couldn't be more pleased for you.'

'You've hated me up to date. Go on, confess it.'

'No,' she shook her cloud of dark hair. 'There's no hope for any of us if we hate.'

'You're too generous, Lynda,' he told her. 'You always have been, and we're kind of twisted people.'

'You're straighter than you know,' she assured him.

They stood there with their arms laced around one another, savouring the first moments of real friendship, when Kyle came out of the library and walked towards them, his measuring look rather cool and sardonic.

'I appreciate you looking after Lynda for me, Joel,' he said dryly.

'Very respectfully, brother.' Joel gave a crooked smile. 'Lynda and I have decided to begin again and I want to tell you what I've always known, you have one heck of a wife.' Very simply he bent his head and kissed Lynda's cheek, then they all laughed together with the uncomplicated joy of the moment.

'What was all that about?' Kyle asked her when they were in the car.

'I'll let Joel explain his plans.'

'My God, I hope they're not trouble!'

'Give him a chance, Kyle,' Lynda begged.

'How can you say that?' His voice was low and almost tender. 'I've given Joel more chances than a doting father with his only child.'

'I don't think he's going to create any problems,' Lynda said lightly.

'Give me a clue and I'll see if I can judge.'

'Perhaps I have no right.'

'Tell me, Lynda,' he said, firmly. 'Joel has good reason to trust me.'

She was silent for a moment looking down at the pale glimmer of her hands, then she told him everything that had given rise to Joel's plans. 'So there you are!' she finished off hurriedly, waiting for his comments. Instead it was a few moments before he had anything to say.

'I'd give a lot to see Joel his own man and successful.'

'I, too,' Lynda returned gravely. 'You could never be blamed, of course, but you've rather eclipsed him since the day he was born.'

'Who cares to comfort me?' Kyle shrugged slightly.

'You know what I mean.' She touched his sleeve apologetically.

'Certainly I do.' A cool, ironic smile touched his mouth. 'I hope you can see it's been just as difficult for me as for Joel.'

'You have so much, Kyle,' she said carefully. 'That's why you're always the one who has to endure. So much is expected of you, and because you never let anyone down and you make decisions so easily your family can't seem to bear the idea of cutting themselves free and independent. Like your grandfather, you have so much natural authority, I suppose it's power—you don't realise what effect you have on the people around you.'

'Are you trying to give me the reason for *your* rebellion?'

Lynda flushed at his curt tone. 'Strange, isn't it? I thought you loved me.'

'So the proof of it was to try and destroy me?'

'I could never do that, Kyle. No woman could.'

He smiled with bleak humour. 'You should understand a little more about your own power. While you're analysing me, I'll give you one back. I expected more of you than anyone else in the world, so you can imagine the extent of my disillusionment when you stood us up in a divorce court. To this day you've never given me the truth of it, so I've come to the conclusion you're unbalanced on one point. We have, I believe, a perfect sex life, but you won't talk to me.'

'Please, Kyle, let it rest!' She spread out her hand pleadingly.

'Lock up whatever ruined our marriage behind closed doors,' he told her drily.

'I'll never be able to go to this party, Kyle,' she warned him, the tears gathering in her throat.

'All right.' His dark profile looked blunt and ruthless. 'We'll call a temporary truce, though I rather like you when you're soft and tearful.'

'Despise me, don't you mean?' Anger and a wave of passion hit her at the same time.

'Lynda . . . Lynda!' He took one hand off the wheel and grasped her arm as though he too was plunged into seething emotion.

'I'll have a bruise there, Kyle,' she warned.

'To hell with a few bruises! To hell with you, my torment.'

'I'm afraid I'll never understand you.' Her breath was coming in short rasps.

'Then just be grateful for what you're feeling now.'

His face hardened to granite and he took his hand away.

The effect of their clashing was that they both walked through the entrance of the MacMillans' palatial house with a heated radiance that drew every eye. Kyle looked blazingly handsome as though he was nourished by power and ambition, and the love of his beautiful young wife, and anger and racing adrenalin had lent a fantastic edge to Lynda's looks. Spectacular as was the beautiful creation she wore around her neck, it was only part of her appearance and not the focus of all eyes.

'How lovely to see you, my dear,' Hugh MacMillan, their host and a real estate tycoon famous for his bravura ventures, took Lynda's hands and kissed her cheek. 'Kyle must be in paradise with such a lovely wife.'

Lynda merely smiled sweetly and let it pass. Surely one was only tormented in hell?

The dinner party started with cocktails in the library, and because Kyle had not prepared her, Lynda was shocked to see Olivia had come along with her big, cigar-smoking father and not the docile woman he had married.

Olivia, on the other hand, had had them under surveillance from the very moment they had walked through the door.

'Don't tell me, Kyle and Lynda!' She gave Lynda a dazzling, entirely false smile and in full view of everyone kissed Kyle full on the mouth.

'The privilege of nearly family,' she explained herself gaily.

'You *are* kind!' Kyle told her suavely, whether from immunity or social panache was anyone's guess.

'I'm afraid I hardly see you any more,' Olivia cooed

regretfully, affixing herself very promptly to his arm.

'Will this encourage you to make a few more phone calls?' Lynda asked, and while Olivia was searching for an answer, allowed herself to be drawn away.

Twenty of them sat down to dinner in the large, formal dining room decorated in an appropriately grandiose manner. Hugh MacMillan was a larger than life-size kind of man and his wife, Daphne, unashamedly matched him. The butt of many an unkind joke behind her back, she was, nevertheless, a very pleasant and sincere woman and she was a great deal more shrewd than many people gave her credit for.

'This is my *grand coup de théatre*!' she told her guests rather unnecessarily as they were being shown to their places around the massive mahogany dining room table. Baronial in style, it subdued their brilliant colour scheme of crimson carpet, lots of mirror and gilt and a wealth of crystal wall sconces. Elaborate silver candelabra were ranged down the table interspersed with mercifully low floral decorations and if it all looked a trifle overwhelming it somehow contrived to look comfortable.

'That's Hughie, of course!' Daphne gestured eloquently towards the large portrait that dominated a very dominant room. The kilted 'Hughie' glared down at them, while their genial host smiled.

'It's a long way from a Scottish castle to Queensland, but it transformed my dear Grandad's life. It's a fine thing to know I own more land than all my cousins put together.'

'One thing for sure,' Daphne assured him, 'you look well in the kilt.'

Many of the guests, pretty close to laughing, burst out with it and the party went on very happily from there. To the women's great relief, very little business was discussed and whenever 'Hughie' inevitably lapsed into it, his wife took care to deliver an opening gambit that set him off in quite another direction. As a man who had taken great risks all his life he had many stories to tell and he had a dry and entertaining tongue.

The courses came and went and the conversation ranged over an extraordinary number of diverse subjects; travel, politics, (because they all voted for the same party), the hair-raising adventures of Hughie's youth, a current sensational murder trial, youth and how to preserve it and the undoubted truism that it was wasted on the young, realism in art versus the dubious capacity for greatness of abstract, a dozen other things that kept people interested or laughing or both.

It was not enough for Olivia to await her moment. Flushed with cocktails and more than her fair share of wine she became almost garrulous until her father finally concerned himself and instructed her to 'tone down' with his eyes. Fierce eyes they were too, so even for Olivia it was a chastening experience.

'I think Father is going to read me a lecture,' she smiled, and shrugged her white shoulders deprecatingly. 'Kyle, it's you who's leading me on.'

'I'm so sorry your mother wasn't able to come,' Daphne said gently, unaware that that good lady had been given no choice.

'Now what about coffee in the library?' Hugh heaved himself out of his chair. 'I've saved up some port that's worth drinking.'

As she stood up, Olivia's trailing sleeve caught her fragile, long-stemmed wine glass and swept it on to the carpet where miraculously it came to rest intact. The contents, however, red wine, splashed over

Olivia's bronze and green silk taffeta skirt and she gave a little helpless shriek.

'Mercy!'

'That's a tall order,' Kyle bent quickly and retrieved the crystal wine glass. 'Here, use my handkerchief.'

'Thank you, darling.' Olivia mopped ineffectually.

'What a shame!' Daphne didn't look as distraught as she should have.

'Lynda,' Olivia abruptly fixed the younger woman with her long amber eyes, 'please help me sponge it off.'

'This way.' Daphne waved to them to follow her to the powder room.

'Thank you, Daphne dear,' Olivia murmured in a dismissive, jarringly patronising voice.

'Right, me lady.' Daphne gave a polished performance of an old char.

'Oh, I'm sorry,' Olivia had the grace to apologise. 'I just wanted a few private words with Lynda.'

'Assuredly you do,' Daphne retorted. 'The question is, is Lynda hale enough to take it?'

Lynda laughed, then choked, and in the end Daphne had to get her a glass of water, while Olivia positively gaped at both of them.

'I say, I thought I was the one who needed attention!'

'My dear, you have me literally on my hands and knees.' Daphne turned swiftly to sponging Olivia's beautiful, expensive dress with cold water. 'I have a private stock of Drive if you'd like to take it off.'

'That's fine, thank you, Daphne.' Olivia gave another one of her dismissive waves. 'Naturally I loathe causing a fuss.'

Daphne's humorous blue eyes rested meaningfully in Lynda's, then she turned to the door of her suffocatingly pink powder room and smiled. 'Don't be long now, girls. We're still a party.'

'Odd woman, isn't she?' Olivia ventured quite matter-of-factly.

'I like her,' said Lynda firmly.

'She's quite a conversation piece, poor Daphne.'

'So are we all at one time or another.'

'Ah, yes, dear.' Olivia's smooth, good-looking face took on a frightening look of enmity. 'It's amazing how often you've been singled out lately.'

Lynda moved back, undismayed. 'People eventually make up their own minds, Olivia. What do you really want to talk about?'

Olivia leaned back against an ornate Victorian console. 'The same old subject—Kyle's folly in adhering to you.'

'Surely he's explained it to you? He refuses to accept failure.'

'Well, this is one fight that he's not going to win.' There was a swift flash of anger in Olivia's golden eyes. 'You didn't survive your first attempt, and I hear things are no better now then they were before.'

'Did Christine tell you that?'

'Well, Christine tells me everything! Didn't you know? Besides,' the predatory eyes narrowed, 'there's Kyle working late long nights in a row.'

'And what you're attempting to convey now is that he's sometimes with you?'

'Sometimes,' Oliva agreed with a smile. 'Isn't it lovely we're all so civilised? I mean, the fairy-tale bit, boy meets girl and they're happy-ever-after is sheer nonsense, as we both know. The fact is, I can't challenge you in your capacity as Kyle's wife, neither can you challenge me as his long-time lover.'

'And you say he's been playing lover to you recently?'

'Force of habit,' Olivia said softly. 'Can't you believe, at least, it's possible for a man to love two women at the same time?'

'Kyle doesn't love you, Olivia,' Lynda said sombrely.

'I'm afraid he does,' Olivia contradicted her flatly. 'I'm necessary to him, otherwise why does he keep coming back to me?'

'If it were true, I'd be wondering that myself,' Lynda said caustically. 'For that matter, how do I know everything you ever told me wasn't one unforgivable fiction?'

'Surely Christine explained the whole thing to you once before?'

'So she did,' Lynda answered quietly, 'but you could have set her up. Christine was the necessary prop and you've always had great influence on her.'

'Scarcely enough to make her lie about something so serious.'

'And infidelity *is* serious?'

'My dear, I'd hardly have reacted any better.' Olivia looked at her with cool pitying eyes. 'I suppose we women, poor creatures, have to accept that we can't be all things to our men. Kyle has a tenderness for you, I know, even a passion. You have a sort of innocent sensuality even I can see, but in many ways you're too simple. I'd like to discuss it with you at length, but right now we simply don't have the time. If you can just love Kyle and accept me, we'll all begin to settle, but if you can't, dare I hope you'll have the sense to get right away from him this time. We all know the old man left you a lot of money. This time it should be easy.'

'Except that Kyle cares too much about holding on

to his marriage and too little about you. I'm sorry for you, Olivia, if that's any help.'

Olivia's reaction was swift and passionate. 'Don't be sorry for *me*,' she exclaimed vehemently. 'Did you know I can't have children? That's why Kyle couldn't marry me.'

'Perhaps it's a mercy,' Lynda responded with extreme difficulty. 'I don't know how you see yourself, Olivia, but I think you're very cruel. Maybe you were an episode in our lives I have to forget about, but I don't believe Kyle has come back to you now. Who knows, I might be older and wiser, but even if you were telling the truth I'd have to endure it.'

'But you couldn't before!' Olivia grasped at her arm, her face working with a kind of desperation.

'There is no release from my marriage, Olivia,' Lynda's voice came back with absolute finality. 'Kyle and I are together until death us do part.'

CHAPTER EIGHT

THE party didn't break up until well after midnight and once in the car Lynda sank back against the leather seat and closed her eyes.

'Tired?' Kyle glanced across at her, leaving the interior light on so he could see her face.

'A little,' she murmured, looking into the deep well of her own fears.

'With your eyes shut you look very poignant, like a Madonna.'

'And with them open?'

'Spring walking down a valley.'

'You could always charm me wth your words,' she said wryly.

'And conquer you with my body,' he added, rather harshly. 'What else has happened in the last few hours?'

'What makes you ask?'

'You're different again. I can't keep up with your changing moods.'

'Can you keep up with two women?' she asked flatly.

'Now what the hell is *that* supposed to mean?' They stayed stationary in the driveway while he shot her a baffled look.

'I'd rather you didn't have intense conversations with Olivia in an empty garden. I'd rather you didn't hold hands with her and allow her to kiss you so greedily like forbidden fruit.'

Unexpectedly Kyle laughed. 'But that's what I am, baby, forbidden fruit, don't you see?' There were headlights in the distance and he pulled out swiftly on to the wide, tree-lined avenue. 'You've got to understand Olivia.'

'And you do?'

'I've known her all my life.'

'Did you ever seriously think of marrying her?'

'Once I did,' he said lightly. 'There were others too, but no one once I met you. Clinically, I suppose, you could call it obsession.'

'And what would you call your relationship with Olivia?'

'Oh, come *on* now!' There was so much amused mockery in his voice Lynda sat up straight and opened her eyes.

'Answer the question,' she insisted.

'My love, I can't believe you're jealous! You're the one woman in the world I thought was free of that terrible, wrenching emotion.'

'I'm not jealous,' she said, which was true. Maimed, raw and bleeding, yes.

'I'm sorry if Olivia has upset you. She's been playing games for so long I simply don't take any notice.'

'You were taking notice in the garden. The light was falling on your face and whatever you were talking about it wasn't very trivial.'

'Most of it was about you,' Kyle assured her.

'How you'd be better quit of me?'

'Impossible. You agreed to the terms.'

'I didn't agree to any conspiracies with other women,' she reminded him.

'And I didn't agree to any luncheon sessions you might think of having with Scott Walker,' he returned drily.

'Don't be ridiculous!'

'Ditto,' he returned tartly. 'What did Olivia say specifically to depress you?'

'What she's been saying for years.'

'Presumably it's something about me. Maybe if I keep questioning you something will emerge.'

'Yes, we might be able to talk like an old married couple.'

'So what did she say?' Kyle asked, his voice quiet.

'She said among other things she could never have children.'

'You know what? One would have to feel glad for the kids.'

'Don't you *care* about her?' Lynda asked passionately. 'It would be a tremendous shock to a woman to know she could never bear children.'

'And Olivia told you she couldn't?'

'She said that was why you would never marry her.'

'I wanted to, of course.'

'Well, of course. You admitted that yourself.'

'Odd she never confided her crushing blow to me,' remarked Kyle.

'You mean you didn't know?' Her voice sounded distant, as though it was coming from very far away.

'I would say, darling, it's her way of getting your attention. As far as I know Olivia is perfectly healthy in all respects except maybe emotionally. But then, who is? Your behaviour might be called neurotic or at the very least disturbed, and I'm struggling to hold a woman I had to blackmail into remarrying me. Incidentally, I've had a progress report on Martin. He's doing extremely well.'

Lynda nodded her head gratefully in response. 'I'm so glad. What Martin did pretty well changed everything, didn't it?'

'Don't sound like I set him up.'

'You would never do that.'

'Thank you.' He flickered a brief, sideways glance at her. 'How come Olivia got on to the subject of my marrying her?'

'Apparently she's never got off it. Did you love her, Kyle?'

'I've always had a fragile affection for her. We grew up together, and that in itself is a bond. She's Anthea's goddaughter, as you know. Grandfather beamed on her because she always took very good care to appear the kind of young woman he would want for his grandson. In general, in those days, she fitted. But no, I was never in love with her as I now know love to be. There was no ecstasy, no agony, no miracle in my life. She was handed to me like a present and I might almost have accepted, only one day I found myself drowning in a pair of smoky grey eyes.'

'You were her lover?'

'Are you going to make me pay for it for ever?'

'I think you should consider my pain,' Lynda said quietly.

'But damn it, *why*?' They were now pulling into their own driveway. 'God, I was nearly thirty when I married you. I'd enjoyed a lot of women. I was free and so were they. Men might be drawn to virgins, but women still prefer an experienced man—and why not? When a woman offers her body it should be handled with ardour and understanding. You surely can't resent the fact that I took what was offered to me. I still could, only I've lost the heart and the mind to even look at another woman.'

Lynda kept her head tilted back and slightly averted. 'These other women, Olivia and the others, were they all before we married?'

'God, Lynda, you make me sound like a sinister character,' he snapped angrily. 'As far as I'm concerned, marriage is a contract, sacred if you like, binding. *You're* the one who broke it.'

In their room Lynda undressed in silence, feeling prey to a hundred confusions. Kyle moved away to the dressing room and she slipped her nightgown over her head and pulled on the matching peignoir. His anger and the words he had chosen had robbed her of the fire of certainty and she had nothing to say.

When he came back into the bedroom he was wearing only black hipster briefs and his lean darkly tanned body had a male grace and virility that still vaguely shocked her. His every movement was so lithe and self-assured, flow of muscle, sheen of skin, the pattern of dark body hair that arrowed into a peak. He was entirely unselfconscious in fact intent on setting the alarm on his beautiful gold watch.

'Could you release the catch on my necklace, please, Kyle?' Lynda asked meekly.

'Sure.' He answered moodily, his eyes a brilliant flash of colour in a sombre, dark face. 'Turn around, my poor sacrificial little lamb.'

For once those sure, steady hands fumbled. 'Obviously this isn't intended to come off.'

She could see their dual reflections in the mirror and he looked like some frowning pagan god, all but naked, while she looked as innocent and vulnerable as a young bride, veiled in draperies of a delicate rose-pink. The décolletage of her nightgown was very low and the glittering necklace took on an added dimension of unintended eroticism.

'*Can't* you do it?' Her mouth began to tremble and her long eyelashes blinked.

'Why don't you leave the damn thing on and take everything else off?'

'I'm tired tonight.' Her voice was so quiet he could hardly hear it.

'Are you, darling?' To her surprise his voice was very gentle, and he turned her and saw the tears in her eyes. 'Lynda.' He bent his head and kissed her eyes and her long black lashes, and when a few escaping tears rolled down her cheeks he took them into his mouth. 'Why do you go in such terror of your own surrender?'

'I still love you, Kyle,' she said shakily. 'Do you know that?'

'No.' Now he was kissing behind her ear, the side of her neck and her throat. 'If you loved me you would talk to me, confide in me, but you hug to yourself so many secrets.'

Very slowly, so as not to frighten her, he peeled away the peignoir from her shoulders and though her eyes were very large and a pulse beat frantically in her slender golden throat, she stood very still in total submission. 'If you'd only let yourself,' Kyle said huskily, 'you would learn to love me all over again. It could be like it was in the beginning when we shared every part of our lives deeply. Sure, there was always the family, but we locked them out. Everything, hostilities, resentments, floated around us but never touched down. No one could intrude on what we had. Maybe I was ready for total commitment, but you were so young you weren't ready to face it.'

'I *was*!' she said passionately, her eyes filling with tears again.

'No, darling.' His tender expression turned sombre. 'If you were ready however can you explain the fact that you left me? I still can't get over the shock. It was massive.'

'I thought you didn't love me.' Her voice trailed off. Older now, she had a little understanding of what Kyle might feel had she had been brutally gulled like a green girl. He was a very proud man and he was still very bitter. She didn't think she could dare to tell him she had fled from his supposed infidelity. When it was all said and done she had never, ever, come right out and accused him of anything. That would have been salt to a mortal wound.

'Oh, for God's sake, look at yourself in the mirror!' He spun her so that she had to face her own lost and plaintive expression. 'I did a rotten thing when I forced you into remarrying me. I was even glad when Martin put the two of you in my power. I'm almost like my grandfather, Lynda. I'm prepared to pay any price for what I want. I want *your* love and I want *our* child. I want you to stop taking those birth control pills and let me make you pregnant. A child, a beautiful child of our own, might increase your wellbeing. You've always loved children and so do I. These last months have been a critical time for me. I've had to establish my supremacy if you like, but now everything has settled down and Endco has hopes to do even better. I know you want a home of your own and I know my family are very selfish in their demands, but I feel responsible for them. Perhaps foolishly. In any event, no one means more to me than you. Whatever price you put on your love and loyalty, I'm prepared to pay it. *Whatever* you want, Lynda. I'm not ashamed to beg.'

Her head averted further from him so all he could see was her pure profile and the quick rise and fall of her almost naked breasts under the lace and crêpe-dechine folds. 'Perhaps it's I who should be begging forgiveness of you.'

'I know—I'm *certain*, you've never been involved with any other man.'

'Weren't you angry about Scott?' she almost whispered.

'Look at me, Lynda.' The fingers on her chin forced her head around. He was watching her closely much as an analyst would watch a subject. 'What was it about Walker you found attractive?'

'*Attractive?*' Lynda gave a startled little laugh.

'What drew you to him? Like perhaps a father to a daughter—he was easy to talk to?'

'Easy, yes.' Her large smoky eyes were filled with a faint sadness. 'There were none of the complications of—passion. He just seemed to enjoy my company.'

'So he didn't even attempt to kiss you?'

She flushed and her eyes sparkled. 'Is it the *woman* who isn't allowed to have a lover?'

Kyle shrugged eloquently, looking very male and intolerant, a man would never share. 'You were so young when you lost your parents. I know how much you loved them, the special love you had for your father. Some men can be a father to their wives. You must have found me very demanding—exciting, maybe a little frightening.'

'You're a very exciting man,' Lynda admitted.

'But I wasn't complete for you?'

'You were everything!' she said savagely, and hit him. 'Everything—everything in the world to me.'

'So what went wrong?' He was prepared for her sudden outburst of anger, his arms coming around her swiftly and locking her arching body to him. 'You must tell me, Lynda, so I can never let it happen again.'

When challenged she was shamed; by the truth or the lie.

Either way Kyle would despise her. To have lived with him loving her and then to be condemned without trial would make him so angry she would never earn his forgiveness. To know he had lied to her would be to look forward to a pattern of marriage where he recognised no other code but his own. He had indulged himself, however carelessly, with Olivia, and he would do so again.

'Oh, to hell with this!' he muttered roughly. 'The only way I can seem to get through to you is take you to bed.'

'And if I don't want to?' Against all her leaping passions, unreasonably she fought him.

'You do, darling,' he said in a flat voice. 'I know everything you like. What's too much and what's too little, the things that make you desperate and what makes you swoon with pleasure. I can open every single petal, but I can't get to your heart.'

Now she was crying in earnest but no longer struggling. She loved him. God, how she loved him!

'You're not going to pretend you don't want me?' he said, and in her distress she swung up her arms and encircled his neck.

'That's right, I want you. Isn't it awful?'

Kyle lifted her then, aware there was some tragedy going on behind her lovely tear-stained face, but roused himself to the point when they could talk no longer.

Could there be anything in the world more complicated or mysterious than a woman? The mental separation would have been intolerable but for this glittering, abiding, physical passion. It was obvious she desperately needed him to make love to her and so he accepted; their own private heaven and hell.

The only thing, he thought bitterly, he couldn't get cynical about. His own computers could have provided him with the perfect mate, outlook and interests, but the heart settled on the beloved with no regard for things like survival. Love, he reasoned savagely, was the most dangerous disease of all.

Once directed on his course, Joel soon discovered he really was an Endfield after all. The family saw very little of him, but there were absolutely no complaints. As Anthea put it: 'After thirty years of wishing Joel would find himself, I think he finally has.'

'You're happy, aren't you?' Lynda caught him one morning as he was hurrying out to his car.

'I am, Lynda.'

'I'm glad,' she told him.

'I know you're glad, sweetie,' he said briskly, though he was really very moved. 'Don't you realise this mightn't have happened but for you?'

Christine stood at the top of the stairs watching them, obliged to admit the truth of that statement, persecuted by her own miserable thoughts. What she needed was the confessional, but she was convinced no god would forgive her.

Downstairs Lynda and Anthea were discussing the arrangements for a reciprocal dinner party the invitations were going out for by the weekend.

'Hi!' Lynda said as Christine walked into the sun-filled morning room.

'Good morning, Lynda,' Christine said quietly, but it sounded like a cry of despair.

'Anything wrong, dear?' Anthea allowed her half-moon glasses to slip down her nose. 'You look pale.'

'I'm wondering how I can improve my life.'

'Why not do as Joel did!' Anthea offered crisply. 'Take Lynda's advice.'

Christine collapsed into a chair and both women wondered at her uncharacteristic look of softness and vulnerability. 'I think what Olivia said to me put an end to any feeling of friendship and loyalty I had for her.'

'And what exactly did she say?' Anthea asked angrily, the mother-tigress in defence of her cub. 'You never would tell us.'

'She was very cruel,' Christine said slowly. 'She always took care to make me feel like *someone*, but that time she slipped up. It was Lynda's suggestion, you see, and she's insanely jealous of Lynda.'

'How could she be?' Anthea asked calmly.

'Oh, Mother!' Christine shook her head. 'Do you ever bother to see anything that's not pleasant?'

'Well, there's no good being jealous of Lynda,' Anthea said defensively. 'I mean, Olivia can't be such a fool she'll spend any more time daydreaming about Kyle? She ought to marry someone else at once. Good gracious, some people might think she was over the hill! Even the idea I suppose we all had of Olivia as family seems terribly remote. We must have been entirely different people.

'We *are* different people since Grandfather's gone,' Christine said with bitter irony. 'Take you, for instance, when did you ever allow admirers to take you out to dinner?'

'Teddy is an old friend,' Anthea protested, and blushed like a young girl. 'As you know very well, he was our best man.'

'And he's been in love with you since before then,' Christine laughed harshly. 'Oh, don't worry, Mother! You're all grown up. Grandfather isn't here to disapprove. You're a beautiful woman, and God knows you've had a raw deal from life.'

'My dear child I've had the best of everything.'

'But the most beautiful, natural thing in the world, a loving man by your side. I don't know how you ever survived losing Daddy.'

'I don't think I actually did.' Anthea sat quite still and the lines of her face sharpened. 'I suppose, really, I stopped growing. In a sense a bit part of my life died with Richard. But I had you, and Joel and Kyle, a living reminder of my husband. He has my eyes, but he's Richard.'

'Not Grandfather?'

'Never Grandfather,' Anthea said emphatically. 'He has all Grandfather's powers, but Richard's harmonious mind and body. Kyle is a compassionate man. Dear Grandfather wasn't, nor did he ever pretend to be. Still, in his fashion, he was very good to all of us.'

'Excuse me if I don't agree.'

'But then you find it difficult to agree about anything,' said Anthea, and swept up, obviously upset.

'Mother?' Christine put out her hand beseechingly, but Anthea, tall and supple, hurried by.

'Forget it. I'm fine.'

'Why is it that everything I mean to say gets out of control?' Christine asked bitterly of Lynda.

'You're unhappy,' Lynda said. 'Unhappy people tend to strike out, but they hurt themselves as much as they hurt anyone else.'

'Oh, my God, don't they!' Christine muttered with a shudder. 'Have you ever in your life wanted to hurt anyone, Lynda?'

'Kyle occasionally,' Lynda smiled. 'You know the way the song goes, you always hurt the one you love . . .'

'Have you ever told wicked lies?'

'No.' Lynda shook her head.

'That was very positive,' Christine said gravely. 'Back in a flash.'

'I don't like hurting people, Christine,' Lynda said persuasively. 'I hope I'm never capable of telling a destructive lie, but I suppose it *could* happen when emotions become too strong for us.'

'I've lived a wicked lie about my own brother,' Christine said baldly. 'The brother I adore.'

'And it's troubling you terribly?'

'Yes. It has for a very long time now, but only lately I've allowed myself to admit it. People avoid the dark places in their souls.'

'What is it?' Lynda asked.

'But you know, don't you?'

'This isn't a dream, is it, Christine?' Lynda asked painfully.

'A nightmare that was always there,' Christine cried in a harsh voice that held back sobbing. 'It wasn't a lie at the beginning. I thought it wasn't. *Please* believe me.' Her hand came out as though to seize Lynda's, but Lynda withdrew like a woman who had to hold in her suffering. 'Olivia was so clever and I was years younger, after all. Olivia used to confide lots of things in me. I was so tremendously flattered. She's so good-looking and witty and sophisticated, and other people found her so . . . worldly, so experienced. There was never a time when she wasn't madly in love with Kyle, and they did seem very close for a while.'

The frenzied words were like the beatings of wings against Lynda's sensitive ears and she almost brought up her hands to protect them. 'Of course,' she said numbly. Everything fell into place.

'I *believed* her, Lynda.' Christine cried beseechingly. 'I thought this was where she belonged. With Kyle. *You* were the usurper, a young girl like myself, yet we were all terrified of you. Even Grandfather. You see, you held Kyle in the palm of your hand.'

'Yet when Olivia told you she and Kyle were lovers you believed her?'

'She showed me pictures of them going into a motel. She said they often spent a night here or there, anywhere they weren't known. It was impossible for him to bring her here, and of course she lived at home.'

'So on the basis of a photograph you swallowed her story hook, line and sinker?'

'Didn't *you*?' Christine darted her a look that was agonised yet triumphant. 'You believed every word I said.'

'You told me, Christine, you'd seen with your own eyes.'

'I'd seen them together, of course,' Christine said evasively.

'Making love?'

'Oh, don't look at me like that, Lynda!' Christine jumped up, ran off a few paces and covered her eyes. 'I was just the sort of jealous pawn Olivia needed. It wasn't for a long time after the divorce that I began to wonder if Olivia had lied. Kyle was distraught, but then many men have no difficulty leading double lives. Olivia was always throwing herself at him and he was human enough to take her, even if he loved you.'

'Your own brother!'

'Your own husband,' Christine reminded her.

'Both of us guilty of an unforgivable sin,' Lynda said with a tragic, twisted smile. 'Did Olivia actually admit she lied?'

'She was proud of it,' Christine said, still sickened. 'All's fair in love and war, she quoted me when I was ready to smash her smiling face to pieces. I'll never forgive her, and I can't forgive myself.'

'Well, I forgive you, Christine,' Lynda said with a deathly sigh. 'Why should you support a cross that was really of my own making? Kyle told me over and over how much he loved me. He proved it in every way. We were so sublimely happy, yet I was used like a fool. I believed, like you, the lies of a cruel and vicious woman against my husband's consistent, loving behaviour. I knew him to be a proud man, a man of honour, yet I broke up my marriage, just like that.'

'You weren't to be blamed!' Christine protested. 'You reacted with the intensity of your own love. I suppose you must feel more deeply than most people. Kyle always said you were deeply sensitive. It's easy to deal with sensitive people, if you know how.'

'And you did, and so did Olivia.'

'God forgive me.' Now, at last, Christine wept, while a few feet away from her, Lynda slid into a deep faint.

A visit from the doctor gave her a shock.

'You're pregnant, Lynda,' he said, beaming at her.

'I can't be!'

'My dear, you are.'

'But I'm not sick. I haven't put on an ounce of weight.'

'Early days yet.' He patted her hand comfortingly. 'Kyle, dear child, will be thrilled. I must confess I am myself. You mean you really had no idea?'

Lynda shook her head as though she could scarcely believe what was happening to her. 'I've never ever followed the normal pattern, so I didn't worry.'

'My goodness!' Dr Stirling never ceased to be startled by women's revelations. 'You weren't using a contraceptive?'

'You gave them to me to regulate things, but I

stopped taking them, as I told you.'

'My goodness, Lynda,' he repeated, then plunged into telling her what she must do to look after herself.

'Afterwards Anthea and Christine came into the bedroom looking rather scared. 'Everything all right, dear?' Anthea asked rather tremulously, 'Colin said it was.'

'I gave her a great shock,' Christine said, still red-eyed and tearful.

'Pull yourself together, dear,' Anthea advised tartly. '*Lynda* is the patient.'

'Patient, nothing!' Lynda protested. 'I'm quite all right.'

'Oh, please lie there, dear,' said Anthea with the utmost concern. 'Sometimes you get a very frail look. I think I should ring Kyle.'

'No.' Lynda put out a staying hand. 'Don't bother him now. It was just a faint.'

'And I'm to blame.' Christine's voice rose in urgent pleading. 'I *have* to tell Mother, Lynda. I have to, or I'll go crazy!'

'You'll go crazy elsewhere,' Anthea said with great coldness. 'Doesn't it trouble you that Lynda is deathly pale?'

'Sit down, Christine,' said Lynda, no resentment in her but little compassion either. Two wasted years. Two terrible wasted years. The pain and humiliation she had inflicted on Kyle, the agony she had done to herself. There was no satisfaction in bitterness or revenge and she didn't seem capable of hardening her heart against the now desolate Christine.

'What *is* all this?' Anthea asked with a curiously pathetic gesture of her hand.

'Christine will tell you,' Lynda said tiredly, and turned her face to the wall.

Afterwards Anthea sat on, chilled to the bone. 'I wonder whether I'm not to blame for everything,' she said with great sadness.

'Of course you're not, Mother.' Christine's voice was tight and low. 'You don't understand how much I love you. I've never been able to tell you.'

'You couldn't confide in me either. Had you even spoken a word, none of this would have happened.'

'I know you'll never forgive me.'

'The question is, will Lynda, will Kyle?'

'Lynda forgives me,' Christine said bleakly.

'Why should I not?' Lynda heaved herself into a sitting position and rested back against the pillows. 'Look at what *I* did.'

'But Kyle loved you frantically, my dear.' Anthea didn't seem able to digest it all. 'Everything he did, he said, was a declaration of his love. It proved it over and over, yet Olivia and my daughter could make you believe he was enjoying some sordid affair on the side.'

'Oliva is very convincing, Mother,' Christine said with terrible self-contempt. 'She mightn't have been a match for you, a mature woman, but she sure deluded two girls. My only excuse, and it's a poor one, is that I really believed her.'

'And even if you *had* you thought you had the right to break up your own brother's marriage?'

'I'd like you to remember, Mother, that we all preferred Olivia to Lynda at that time. We accepted her as a very stylish and sophisticated young woman, one who had entry to this house from the very beginning. What we didn't know was that she would resort to any strategy, however low. She used me because I was, and still am, a great fool.'

'And mine is the greater blame,' Anthea said despairingly, looking in an instant about ten years older. 'If you'd only come to me with the story I could have put an end to Olivia's lies. Did you not understand Kyle had gone far beyond Olivia even before he met Lynda? After that, there could be no one. I know my son.'

'And I was too young and too jealous to make the right diagnosis,' Christine said.

Without being aware of it they all lapsed into their own troubled thoughts. All of them wondering how they could ever tell Kyle.

'Why don't we have a cup of tea?' Lynda said at last.

'Tea, dear?' Anthea lifted her head.

'I would say it will make us all feel better.'

'What a terrible business,' sighed Anthea, still looking drawn.

'Then we'll all have to undertake to put it in the past.'

'*Can* you, Lynda?' Christine asked.

'I have to. We all have to. Besides,' Lynda added calmly, 'I'm going to make it all come right. I'm pregnant.'

For a full moment both Anthea and her daughter looked at her blankly, then their faces lit up like sinners faced with salvation. 'But my dear child!' Anthea began to laugh, a wobbly laugh that could have spilled over into tears. 'I'm absolutely thrilled!' She went forward, bent down and kissed Lynda on the cheek. 'Thrilled, believe me. You know, I've waited a long time for a grandchild.'

'And you'll have to be the most glamorous grandmother in the world.'

'Glamour nothing! I'll be gentle and kind and loving, and you can be sure you'll have the house all to yourself. Kyle and I have had a long talk and I've decided I'll live at our coast house, and I daresay you can always look after me when I come into town. Christine will come with me, or we'll find her a nice apartment, and I think you'll find Joel is already making his own arrangements. It's going to be as it should have been from the beginning.'

'I'm so glad for you, Lynda.' Christine, too, approached the bed. 'So long as I live I won't forget what I did to you.'

'I think we will.' Lynda put out her hand and Christine took it.

'You've only seen the worst of me, Lynda, now you're going to see the best. Certainly my little niece or nephew can confidently hope for a wise and affectionate aunt.'

'Now what about that tea?' Anthea said briskly. 'One longs all one's life for happiness, and after much stumbling, I think we've come across it.'

Lynda's news was accepted as a privileged confidence, with Lynda finding the right private moment to tell Kyle when in fact it was destined to come out in a wild tumble.

'I think I'll take a run over to the house,' Lynda told Anthea, late that same afternoon. 'I'm going to give it to Martin.'

'Martin will certainly be very glad of it,' Anthea said. 'Would you like some company?'

'Aren't you going out with Edward this evening?' Lynda asked smilingly.

'Dear old Teddy!' Anthea yawned with the complacency of the born beauty. 'He's always been in love with me, you know.'

'These days I think he's hoping to do something about it.'

'Exactly,' Anthea agreed rather dryly. 'I think I'm

too old for love and all that.'

'When it's the best beauty treatment in the world?' Lynda asked slyly.

'One of the penalties of being an Endfield was that I was never expected to remarry. My place was with Grandfather and the children. For years my grief was so strong I had no need of a man for company or anything else, now I seem to be going into my second girlhood.'

'Edward is a very fine man,' Lynda could say sincerely.

'And he stayed a bachelor just for me!'

The drive to her old family home was a short one and immediately she arrived Lynda opened up the windows and doors to allow the circulation of fresh air through the house. She had not, as yet, told Martin about her plans to give it to him when he was ready to settle down and she was conscious that it might remain empty for some time. Martin might be working well, but he had a long way yet to go before Kyle or Lynda were thinking of rewarding him. She didn't want to let it, neither could she bear to sell it. Since she had married the grounds were kept in an immaculate state by a firm specialising in property service and it was a pleasure to sit out on the verandah with a cold drink and enjoy the beautiful view. The University rowing team were hard at it in preparation for a big race and she leaned back rather dreamily in her planter's chair and watched their smooth progress.

I'm pregnant, she thought, still finding it incredibly strange. The strangest part was that Dr Stirling had had to tell her. She had thought she would have known at once—even the mystical moment of conception, but truly she had known nothing. A baby!

The pleasure, the tears and tenderness was swift. Boy or girl she didn't care. A healthy child. Of course she wanted a son, but she just knew how much she would love a little girl. She decided then and there to have three children—three beautiful children she would take good care to bring up as useful, caring citizens with a developed sense of responsibility. She would be a good mother. Her children would love and trust her. Lynda smiled and rubbed her flat stomach, already communicating with her child. She wasn't Lynda any more, but Lynda and child. The guardian angel to her baby!

Peace began to spread through her. There was no sense in remaining miserably disappointed in herself. She had made some terrible mistakes, but with God's grace she could see a bright future. They all had to learn from today. Over lunch, Christine had spoken of enrolling for a course at the Cordon Bleu School of Cookery in Paris. A graduate of London, it never hurt to pick up another trophy. She had to do something with her days and she really did have talent.

'God knows where she gets her love of cooking from!' Anthea had remarked wryly. 'It must be some hidden gene.' Used to the best of everything, Anthea had nevertheless kept to a stringent diet for years. Hence the superb figure.

Would Kyle be as suddenly thrilled and excited as she was? As Anthea and Christine genuinely were. She desperately wanted him beside her; here in the drowsy, golden late afternoon, the high dazzle of midday gone, the birds flying and Sam, the next-door cat, sitting like a sleepy sphinx on one of the broad stone steps leading down to the lower terrace. Cats were sacred to the ancient Egyptians. They even built temples to them and buried them in gold coffins. Sam

was an old friend. He had even come up to say hello to
Lynda. The gardening firm had worked wonders with
the landscaping. The banks of flowering shrubs were
all there, but so beautifully restrained, the old walks
had been redefined and the pergola mended and
repainted. Kyle had once come over to check on what
was being done and stayed to sit around and admire.
He had so little free time. She would have to make
each leisure moment precious.

Sunset was beautiful, the sun sloping down through
incandescent pink and gold cloud blent with amethyst.
Lynda couldn't decide which was the best part of the
day, dawn or sunset. It would soon be winter, the
brilliant, warm blue and gold of Queensland. No
expatriate Australian ever seemed able to reconcile
themselves to the climate of the rest of the world, and
with good reason. Australia *was* the sun, and even
Australians flocked to the winter sun of Queensland.
Her baby would arrive when the jacarandas and the
poincianas were coming into bloom. It would be their
most beautiful Christmas.

She didn't even hear the car until it was almost two
feet from her own car, and when she saw *what* car it
was, she jumped up at once, filled with a kind of alarm.

Scott Walker was advancing towards her, tall and
distinguished-looking, his usually reserved face rather
flushed over the cheekbones, his eyes shining with
some kind of pent-up emotion.

'Lynda—ah, I'm so glad to see you're all right!' The
words came out in a rush and he came up the stairs
holding out his two hands. 'Now tell me what's the
matter?'

'The matter, Scott?'

'I got your message.' He looked deeply into her
widened eyes. ' I came at once.'

Lynda was shocked by the eagerness on his face. 'I sent no message, Scott,' she said quietly.

'But you did!' He gave a lopsided grin. 'I was to meet you here at the house. You had something important to tell me.'

'Please sit down, Scott.' She turned quickly, feeling dizzy, and sat down herself. 'Someone is obviously playing a joke on us.'

'What kind of a joke?' Scott asked sharply. He sat down beside Lynda and grasped her hand. 'You've gone very white.'

'I'm all right.'

'My dear, you've lost all your lovely colour. You looked so ... peaceful when I arrived. As if you'd come to some decision. *Have* you?' he asked, with all his heart in his eyes.

'Who gave you the message, Scott?' she asked him.

'Actually my secretary handed it to me. I was on the other line and the lady didn't wait. Naturally when it said Lynda I accepted that it was you.'

'Then it was a ... woman.' Never a lady.

'Yes, of course. 'Scott's rare, boyish smile was drying. 'You didn't ring me, Lynda?'

'No, Scott,' she answered quietly. 'It is, as I said, a malicious joke.'

'But who would *do* such a thing?' He looked shocked.

She shrugged moodily. '*I* know.'

'Would it be too much to ask you to tell me?' Scott gave her a swift, frowning look.

'The same woman with the sick mind. Olivia Dowling.'

Scott digested this cautiously. 'How would she think of *me*?'

'Olivia is more than a match for either of us when it

comes to malice and intrigue. Maybe she's just making some happy little diversion for herself, or maybe she's intending worse trouble.'

'Such as?' Scott, always a conservative man, looked thoroughly alarmed.

'I don't think we'll wait to find out.' Lynda stood up quickly. 'I didn't ring you, Scott, but I do appreciate that you came to possibly help me out. You go. Get away from here while I shut the house. I only came over to air it, in any case.'

'I'll help you,' Scott said gallantly. 'All the windows are open—I noticed that immediately.'

'All right,' Lynda gave him a grateful glance. 'You start at the front of the house and I'll go to the back.'

They met a few minutes later in the darkening hallway. 'This is rather a vulgar business,' Scott said unhappily. 'I mean, you're a married woman.'

'Didn't you know that, Scott, before you came?'

'Yes, yes—vulgar was too harsh. I would do anything in any case to help you. Tell me you're happy?'

'I'm happy, Scott.' She looked up at him and he became suddenly emotional and grasped her shoulders.

'I got what I asked for, didn't I, coming here?'

'I'm sorry, Scott,' Lynda said poignantly. 'So sorry. Some people are very, very cruel.'

'I think I'll always love you,' he said, more calmly.

'Well, there's a good cure for that!'

He had come up on them so silently, nothing could minimise the shock.

'*Endfield!*' Scott exclaimed, appalled.

'Who else?'

They were further startled by the terrible menace of his tone and unnatural demeanour. Lynda found herself thinking of a crouching panther ready to strike. So too, apparently, was Scott. His hands had fallen away instantly from Lynda's shoulders and he retreated to the comparative safety of a tall Gothic chair.

'I'd like to explain what I'm doing here.'

'I'd like you to,' Kyle invited him with more than a hint of murderous humour.

'*I'll* tell him, Scott.' Lynda put her slender body between them, but Kyle put his hands on her shoulders and firmly moved her aside.

'Someone sent me a message that Lynda wanted to see me,' Scott burst out hastily.

'Someone sent me a message as well.'

'What did yours say?' Scott asked ingenuously.

'We'll start on your message first.' Kyle lifted a hand and turned on the light. 'Understand that I'm *this* much away from breaking your neck.'

'He only wanted to help,' Lynda cried emotionally.

'I'm very touched.'

'Oh, please, Kyle!' He didn't look at her, but shook his dark head. 'Walker here owes me an explanation.'

'So I'm in love with Lynda!' Scott shouted, sick with humiliation. 'Nothing has ever happened between us.'

'You're damned right!'

'I wish her nothing but happiness, but so far she hasn't been very happy with *you*.'

Kyle gave a brief laugh with no humour in it. 'So you're here to try your luck?'

'I'm here to help Lynda, that's all,' Scott said with dignity. 'I was told she wanted to see me. We had a good friendship, you know. She has a claim on me. In fact, she could ask me anything.'

'Do you think I could ask you to *go*, Scott?' Lynda

swooped towards him and grasped his arm. 'I did not send the message, and I very much regret that you've been caught up in all this.'

'Shall I start the violins?' Kyle asked suavely, and it dawned on Lynda that he had lost a lot of his terrifying demeanour.

'Forgive me,' Scott said stiffly.

'My friend, you're very fortunate there's nothing to forgive,' Kyle told him curtly, in that moment looking very much like his late, ruthless grandfather.

'An awkward situation all around.' Scott clasped his hands together unhappily.

'And a parting one,' Kyle added acidly. 'Allow me to show you to your car. I'm hoping you might tell me something else.'

'Thank you, Scott,' Lynda called after them compassionately.

'I'm sure that's a great help.' Kyle gave her tragic beauty a dry glance. 'Wait right there, Lynda. I'll be back presently.'

In fact he was longer than she expected, but when he came in it was to a whistling chorus of Onward, Christian Soldiers.

'I hope you weren't *too* unkind to him,' she asked accusingly, fired to an aggressive recklessness by his complete volte face. But seriously, how could he be whistling when he had half frightened the life out of her?

'Oh, so-so,' he said calmly, 'considering how I started out.'

'You gave me a terrible fright!'

'Darling,' he said dryly, 'I don't think you know just how much I prize you. I know Walker has an elderly charm, but he's no longer allowed to even look at my wife. *I think I'll always love you, Lynda*!' he breathed soulfully.

'Oh, shut up!' Now it was her turn to be angry.

'But, darling, you're so lovely. I even love you myself.'

'Do you? That's news.' Pale cheeks flushed and she looked very beautiful and stormy.

'Do you mean you're complaining because I don't actually say the words, I love you?'

'Damn you, don't be supercilious with me!' she snapped.

'Can you say it to me?' There was the same old arrogant tilt to his head, the sapphire eyes unwavering.

Lynda swung about, skirt swirling, not even knowing where she was going.

'What a little firebrand!' Kyle caught her up, smiling down into her ominous, stormy eyes. 'Aren't you going to tell me what all this mischief is about?'

'Who gave you your message?' she demanded.

'It was supposed to have come from home.' His voice hardened and the sparkling mockery died out of his eyes. 'You wanted me to meet you at the house. As it turned out, I walked out of an organised meeting.'

'I'm sorry.' She sighed on a wave of remorse.

'Do that again,' he begged her. 'The little helpless sigh. It's charming.' His hand closed under her chin, turning her face up. 'Why, Lynda?' The mockery melted into the most exquisite concern. 'What's the matter, darling?'

'Why shouldn't I be upset?' She leaned forward and laid her head along his chest. 'I hate malice and ugly people. People who want to destroy.'

'You won't ever be upset again,' he said tautly, 'Of that I can assure you.'

'But how do we know who it was?' she whispered carefully.

'Who else could it be?' he said quietly, smoothing her hair. 'Stay like that, my lovely girl. Just let me hold you.'

'I *love* you, Kyle,' she said. The most immensely healing words in the world.

'And I love you,' he answered gently. 'How did we ever lose one another?'

It was the time to confide in him, even as she knew she had to keep Christine's part out of it.

It was, on the whole, much easier than she expected. Kyle sat down in the armchair with her on his lap while she spoke of those terrible days and what had driven her into leaving him. 'I was a fool,' she said at last. 'A naïve girl.'

'My God!' He seemed more stupefied than angry, and terribly hurt. 'You mean you rejected me completely on Olivia's word?'

'You're not to be angry, do you understand!' She tried to put her arms around him and grip him tight. 'I don't think I'll be able to bear it if you're angry with me. I've suffered enough.'

'My God!' he said again, drawing the words out slowly.

'Oh, darling, I've hurt you dreadfully, haven't I?' She began to cry.

'I feel as though I've been trampled by a horse,' he muttered.

'Tell me where. I'll kiss it better.'

'Here.' He hit his heart.

'I never had the sense or maturity, Kyle.' She rubbed her cloudy head back and forth on his chest. 'I couldn't even stay to fight back.'

'Oh, don't,' he groaned. 'This doesn't bear thinking about.'

'We *must* think about it!' She was dampening his

beautiful shirt and silk tie with her tears. 'We can't hold it in.'

'My dearest baby,' he kissed her fingers. 'You held it in for two years.'

'Two lost and really frightening years.'

'How frightening?' His voice was quite different.

'Shall I show you?' Lynda looked up and blinked.

'You better make it good.'

And good it was. Better. She was able to show him completely what he meant to her.

At last it was dark.

'Shall we go home or stay here?' Kyle asked dreamily, as thoroughly exalted as she was.

'I'm hungry.'

'Really?' He looked down at her in surprise. 'You're not usually hungry after we make love.'

'Only now,' she smiled radiantly, 'I'm beginning our child.'

'*Lynda!*' He tried to sit up but had to fall back again, the back of his hand along his eyes. 'Are you telling me you're *pregnant*?'

'Are we going to have a boy or a girl?' Now she was the one who was completely fit and strong.

'But, darling, I've just made love to you violently.'

'And you probably will again.'

'I should have been careful. Oh, God, I can't take this in.'

'I'm pregnant and you have to take care of me.' She pushed his arm away and began kissing him all over the face.

'All these weeks you've been pregnant?'

'Darling,' she lifted her head and looked down at him, 'don't get in such a state!'

'I don't think I'm going to be able to handle this being a father. I mean, you're such a little thing!'

Kyle's densely blue eyes looked dazed.

'Then if it's a boy he'll have to take after you. Petite girls are in order.'

'We're going to have a child!'

'Yes.' She smiled at him with great, luminous eyes. 'I've never been so happy in my life.'

And it was true. The joy was pouring into her, visible in her radiance.

'My little love!' Kyle put out his hand and she went back into his arms. 'I don't think I will kill Olivia after all,' he said simply.

'We can afford to be generous. Just strike her off our visiting list.'

'I'll take care of it,' he said with a fleeting return to hard authority. 'Creatures like Olivia can't intrude on what we've got now. I feel lightheaded with joy.'

For a moment they lay closely twined together, not speaking, then he bent his head and kissed her so deeply, so passionately she was left dazed and speechless. Was it possible to improve upon perfection?

From utter quietness they were swept again into blinding rapture, the whole universe lit with stars, beautiful beyond imagination, the incomparable country of true love.